GLAMOUR

Alexandra and Sophia,
Remember true glamour
resides within.
Enjoy!
Brandi Barnett

GLAMOUR

━━━━━━━━━━━━━━━━

BRANDI BARNETT

HAWK
PUBLISHING
G R O U P
Tulsa, OK

LIBRARY OF CONGRESS CATALOG-IN-PUBLICATION DATA

Barnett, Brandi
GLAMOUR
ISBN 978-1-930709-68-3
Library of Congress Control Number: 2008927837
Copyright © 2008 by Brandi Barnett

Hawk Publishing Group Edition 2008

Cover and interior design: nbishopsdesigns@cox.net
Author photograph by: Wendy Mutz, www.mutzphotography.com

Published in the United States by HAWK Publishing Group

HAWK Publishing Group
7107 South Yale Avenue #345
Tulsa, OK 74136
918-492-3677
www.hawkpub.com

HAWK and colophon are trademarks belonging to the HAWK Publishing Group.

Printed in the United States of America.
9 8 7 6 5 4 3 2 1

ACKNOWLEDGEMENTS

Many patient people have helped make my fairy tale come true. Thank you…

Garrett, for believing in me when I didn't.

Mama and Daddy, for showing me the beauty of life in rural Oklahoma. Brett, for helping me figure out the science stuff.

My writing group The Inklings (Martha Bryant, Kelly Bristow, Dee Dee Chumley, Sonia Gensler, Lisa Marotta), for your inspiration and encouragement with "the fairy story."

Shel Harrington, for your expertise.

Joan Rhine, James Vance, and Jenni Stout, for your generous line editing.

Dr. Connie Squires and her class, for helping reexamine the first ninety pages.

Sara Hoklotubbe and Ange Bunner, for offering an American Indian perspective.

Mika Calico and Aunt Martha Rose Calico, for sharing about the Little People. And Mika and Lisa, for giving your children inventive names that I can use for characters.

Caitlin Graham, for teaching me I'm not too old to indulge in dreams.

K.D. Wentworth, for being an enlightening editor.

Nancy Bishop, for creating the perfect cover art and book design.

Bill Bernhardt, for your guidance and passion for the written word.

AUTHOR'S NOTE

Kat's web searches can really be found. The npr.org article about miniature people exists.

FOR GARRETT

PROLOGUE

She liked to keep their tongues in her pocket. It warmed her soul to know they would never spit or communicate again. She carried their tongues like a talisman, sewn together with fishing line, the holes pierced with a paperclip. At night she placed them on a shelf, secreted behind her book of fairy tales.

Carefully planning her next acquisition, she dipped her finger into the creek, creating ripples. No one could discover her secret or she'd be forced to stop. And her work must continue.

"Katrina!" Cold fingers gripped her arm and jerked her to her feet. "Kat, I called you an hour ago."

"I'm sorry, Mommy." She twirled a pigtail. "I was just playing."

"We're late to your doctor's appointment, and we must get those *hideous* warts removed from your hands." Her mother turned on her heel and headed home.

Lagging behind, Katrina patted the pocket of her Osh-Kosh overalls and muttered, "We won't have to worry about warts much longer. Grandpa said that frogs give you warts—so I'm taking care of them." She smiled. "Kat's got their tongues."

CHAPTER 1

EIGHT YEARS LATER

Blaezi pouted beneath the shade of a dandelion with her chin nestled between her knees. Her long green hair changed to brown as it grazed the earth beneath her. *Why do I have to be the Garden Guard? I never get to do anything fun.* She had been told that the yumsies, Faye caterers, had discovered a stash of M&Ms and she had been looking forward to the feast. She hoped her friends saved her one. Maybe two.

Slowly a fat, pallid grub struggled to the surface of the tilled garden, inches from Blaezi. It looked around before receding back into the moist soil. A few inches closer, the head emerged again, then retracted its body once more. The ground shifted near Blaezi and forced her body against the stem of the dandelion. Puffs of white seeds sprinkled the air as she held tightly to the leaves. The creature wriggled out of the dark underground, and Blaezi looked in his ugly little eyes.

"Rottus, I'm warning you. Go home!" Not giving the small-brained larva time to decide, she pulled a satchel of salt she kept tied around her neck and threw it at the grub. As he shrank in pain from the salt particles, she scrambled to stand and grabbed her weapon.

"Go away, you slimy snazzle!" she shouted at the worm as it squished its way toward her. "Just because the other guards got leave to go to the festival doesn't mean I can't take care of you myself."

Like many Fayes, part of her uniform consisted of items found where humans linger. From her wrists to her elbows she wore silver chewing gum wrappers, fashioned into sleeves. She caught the sunlight with them and directed it at the intruders. Lunging forward, she held her toothpick spear and thrust the weapon at the blinded worm. The point barely missed the filthy side of Rottus. Momentarily he disappeared and she felt earth move beneath her again. Cold dampness of another worm wound its body around Blaezi's left ankle and pulled backward and down. Her body plunged and her face thumped into the dirt.

"Let go, Blight, or I'll give you a real reason to hide underground!" She spat chunks of mud as the words flew from her mouth. She shook the dirt from her wings and, with a grunt, flew upward. As the remaining rays of the hot day's sun hit the grubs' exposed bodies, they released her and fell to the moist earth.

Hovering inches above the ground, she unwound her harshest garden weapon. Around her waist, she wore a tightly knit chain of grass. Dangling from the chain, a dried cocklebur hung. Blaezi released the cocklebur mace from her belt and flung the ball into the air. With each swing, she flew higher until, with decisive precision, she swept to the garden gaining extra momentum from her altitude. She swung at Rottus first. The blow knocked him out of the earth, his body somersaulting sideways until he hit the thick stalk of a sunflower.

Rottus mumbled, "Wugdetung. Wugdetung!" and the grubs disappeared into the earth, but not before Blaezi took a few more whacks at their retreating white tails.

"Yalli-hoo!" Blaezi yelled, fluttering above the dirt. "And don't you come back! Tell all your grimy friends that this is a holiday and to take the day off!" She landed on a ripe tomato and sprawled her body across it.

The sun had completely set and the full moon's rays filled

the summer air with an iridescent glow. A cool breeze carried the music of the crickets' evening song, but tonight the melody was different. Tonight was Midsummer's Eve and they sang in celebration. Tonight the fairies held a festival. Beyond the trees behind the garden, Queen Tania presided over the joyful gala with plenty of food and dancing for all. Everyone was there — except Blaezi.

"Why do I have to be the Garden Guard?" Blaezi punctuated each word by pounding the tomato with her fists. "My life is so boring." Then, she slowly sat up and her eyes glittered. *I was the first to ask to go to the festival. They should have let me. I could say I thought I had permission. The grubs are such ditzlesnits, they'd never notice I was gone anyway.* And with that excuse, she flew from the garden and into the woods, leaving nothing but a trail of magic.

***

The fortune teller adjusted the scrap of red bandanna around her wizened face. "Not everyone needs to know her future."

"I know *that*." Blaezi's wings flitted in anticipation. "That's why I tried so hard to get here by first starlight. I know you won't fortune through the entire Midsummer Festival." She bounced on her knees, the moss cushioning her enthusiasm. "My life needs something exciting to happen. What's my future?"

The teller examined Blaezi, who had turned sterling from top to toes beneath the evening sky. Finally, she said, "Your loyalties will be revealed to all." She pulled her ladybug into her lap and took a long look at its unchanging spots. "The markings stress extreme caution. Your work will send you away. Danger is near you, but trouble will be your guide, salvation, and destiny. You'll have only one chance to find home. You don't recognize the way. Yet."

"Wha...? But...." Blaezi's wings drooped. The seer departed to fortune another Faye.

She felt a hand on her shoulder and turned to see her friend Dion sipping nectar from an acorn cup. "You know you can't argue with a reader or her ladybug," he said. "If she sees your life in its spots, it can't be changed."

Blaezi flew off with Dion shadowing her until she stopped abruptly. Dion swept right into her, knocking her spinning to the ground. As they untangled their wings, her shoulders shook with giggles. "The seer must be wrong. My work didn't send me away. I sent myself away from my work."

"You got the joke on her then!" They slapped a high wing. "Don't think about it anymore, Blaezi. Midsummer Festival only comes once a year." He pointed at a banner announcing just that. By command of the queen, the forest spiders had woven intricate webs above each event creating iridescent signs that glistened with dew and magic.

Blaezi glanced around the forest for their options. Roly-Poly Bowling was nearby, but Blaezi hated picking up the sunflower seed pins after she and her roly-poly knocked them down. At the foot of the North Pine, young Fayes competed in a three-winged race. Blaezi saw their friend Diana at the Magic Tournament, so they zipped off to watch.

Blaezi and Dion wiggled through the crowd. When they reached Diana she asked, "Hey, Blaze, why aren't you on duty in the Garden?"

"Don't get your wings in a wad," Blaezi replied. "What's going on?"

Diana pointed at the competitor whose head had not been transformed into a radish during the transformation round. His garment was only a small fragment of tanned animal hide. "This new guy showed up when the games began, and he was the first to make a challenge... don't you think he's rather handsome?" Diana floated a little higher. "I especially like how his wings are laced with silver."

"I guess he's all right," said Blaezi, "but he's slug-faced compared to Dion."

Queen Tania and her courtiers watched from floating leaf balconies cushioned with cottonwood tufts. She was adorned in a gown of wild canary and cardinal feathers that encircled her body from shoulder to ankle, fanning out into soft plumage of yellows and iridescent blues and greens. They were tied together beneath her chest with a strand of stray ribbon and a red bead collected from the garden. Her jester sat at her feet, dewdrops glistening from the points of his coneflower cap.

The last match of magic sizzled through the sky, leaving the visitor astride his Scissor-tail Flycatcher and the Faye gasping for breath flat on his back, clutching his pine needle lance. Queen Tania applauded the stranger, winner of the jousting round and the entire tournament. After her first clap, the rest of the court followed her lead in cheering the champion.

The jester exclaimed, "You demonstrate great skill with the Glamour. Where do you come from that teaches such tricks?"

The air surrounding the stranger sparkled. He bowed to the queen then flew high into the sky. "My name is Thorne. I am one of the People from Rock River."

Color drained from the queen's face. "Thorne?" She swooned. Several pixies flew to her aid and fanned her with rose petals until she was alert once more. The jester looked as if he'd bitten into a rotten apple.

A titter passed through the crowd. "Rock River!" cried a young Faye whose wings showed the first signs of glimmer. "I didn't know it really existed."

Another one murmured, "No wonder his magic is strong."

"He's a *Natural*?!" Diana's wings failed her. Dion managed to grab her by the ankle before she tumbled to the forest floor.

The stranger hovered above the crowd. "I have a message."

Flickering fireflies took on a steady glow as the forest stilled. All eyes and ears were trained on Thorne, waiting to hear his news.

Then the ruckus began.

A yumsy blared into the forest and shouted, "The Garden has been desecrated!"

The queen snapped her fingers, and two guards gripped the arms of the trembling yumsy. He screamed through the silent night, "But I *serve* the food, not *protect* it!" The queen tilted her head in consideration as the yumsy continued his plea. "Blight and Rottus desecrated the Garden! Holes run through each plant. Vines lie limp against the ground, appearing as only lines drawn on the dirt. The Garden is closed and will not reopen until the change of seasons... if at all."

The wind changed. The queen's eyes narrowed on a wide-eyed figure at the front of the crowd. "Blaezi!" she hissed.

Queen Tania snapped again, and the guards dropped the yumsy in the dirt. Before Blaezi could take a breath, the guards, their fingers piercing her skin like a snake bite, dragged her to face the queen and her court.

The jester asked Blaezi, "Have you been sipping from still waters again?" The queen laughed before glaring at Blaezi, who feared she might be sick.

Queen Tania's voice, barely above a whisper, was as steady as a wasp's wings. "Do you know what you've done?"

"A full day's work?" Blaezi tried to grin and shrug, but the guards' grips were like boa constrictors. "Okay... seriously, Blight and Rottus popped up earlier today while I was on Garden duty."

"Nasty grub worms," muttered the yumsy.

Blaezi nodded her agreement. "I fought the grubs until they surrendered. I figured they wouldn't even notice I was gone, so I left post and came here. Really... who'd have known we needed to worry about them during a party?"

"I imagine someone had a notion," the yumsy said, tugging on his lower wings. "Perhaps that's why you were posted as Garden Guard?"

"Silence!" Queen Tania's anger and volume grew to its full magnitude. "Convene the council! I'll deal with the Natural there." A group of elder Fayes escorted Thorne into a knothole in a large tree. Even the leaves shook as Queen Tania turned back to Blaezi. "Your irresponsibility and lack of thought foretells a difficult summer for everyone here. No pies left on the windowsill to cool. Unattended sweets marked with a cross to keep our People away. Soon, an iron fence erected to repel us. Why?" Her voice became low and even again. "Because you did not uphold our end of the contract. All young Fayes know we guard the Garden of the Mortals from reptiles and insects—especially grubs. In return the humans provide us with all the food we desire. A classic contract, yet you managed to make a debacle of it—as in all that you do." She reached for a leaf of food, then retracted her hand and scowled at the crowd. "Our People will be forced to scavenge for wild berries and honey as if we are some sort of... of *Naturals!*" Queen Tania squinted her eyes to see Blaezi better. "When was the last time you trimmed your tail?"

Blaezi felt heat rise to her face. "Just last week. It grows faster than everyone else's." She hung her head. "I can't help it."

The queen smoothed her golden hair. "You're rarely presentable. You're selfish. You're irresponsible." With disdain, she glanced at the tree where Thorne and the elders had disappeared.

GLAMOUR

"Many on the Council claimed you were the finest guard we had."

"*Were?*" Blaezi asked.

Queen Tania stood and a great burst of Glamour glittered around her, causing many in the crowd to shield their eyes. When the brightness passed, Blaezi noticed three tiny bags of Glamour dangled from her waist instead of weapons.

The queen's voice echoed from every tree. "You are banished."

Blaezi heard her friend Diana sob and the sound punctured her heart. "But I'm your best guard," she pleaded. "You need me." She struggled to free herself from the guards who were already dragging her away. "Wait…. Doesn't Faye law permit me to redeem myself? Don't I have some kind of terms?"

"Very well," Queen Tania said. "I'm nothing if not charitable."

The guards stopped.

"Rid the Garden of Blight and Rottus. Solve whatever problem the Naturals are pestering us about." The queen sighed. "Do these within two moon cycles and you may return."

Blaezi looked down at the small bags around her waist. "I'll need more Glamour."

Queen Tania smiled wickedly. "That's all you're getting from me."

"And how do I know what the Naturals need when he hasn't even told us yet?"

The queen opened her hands to the sky. "That is not my concern."

As guards carried her away, Blaezi looked back for a final glimpse of her friends. Dion and Diana remained motionless, their tear-filled eyes matching her own.

15

CHAPTER 2

Kat scurried to the river to continue her zoology assignment. The majority of her summer school classmates flunked the subject last year and lazily served their time so they could be promoted to 12th grade. Kat, a sophomore-to-be, took the course to get ahead. Science fascinated her almost as much as make-up and fashion.

The final class project was to create a mini-ecosystem and discuss its interactions. Natural elements weren't difficult to find in Eastern Oklahoma, but most of her classmates were cutting pictures from magazines or copying from coloring books and pasting onto poster board. Kat, however, considered a living, captive ecosystem more beautiful and had gathered specimens in her vivarium for weeks.

Although her motivation to hunt had changed over the last eight years, her target was the same today. "Here, froggy, froggy, froggy!" She stalked her prey along the riverbank.

After setting her sack lunch on the grass, she pulled a pink compact from her shorts and opened it. "Mirror, Mirror, in my hand, view who's the fairest in the land." She gazed into her reflection. To anyone—or thing—observing her, she appeared to preen. On the contrary, she used the mirror to study the surrounding environment without arousing suspicion.

Glimpsing moving grasses and water ripples, Kat knew another capture would soon be hers. She lay the open compact beside her lunch and crept on hands and knees toward the movement. When she arrived, though, nothing was there. She flipped over rocks and disrupted the grass to drive out the frog, but nothing appeared. The persistence of her grumbling stomach must have frightened it away, so she decided to eat her lunch instead.

She stretched out on her stomach and munched her midday meal. Careful not to touch the food with her dirty hands, Kat kept her tuna sandwich wrapped with plastic. After eating, she reached for the mirror to resume her work. But her arm stopped mid-air. Sitting on the mirror and staring at its reflection was a creature barely taller than a crayon set on end. Fluttering its wings and prissing this way and that, it appeared to be female. Slender arms and tiny hands fluffed the glittering, grass-colored tendrils of its tail. She was the most beautiful thing Kat had ever seen—almost magical.

In one swift motion, Kat scooped her up in a sandwich bag.

Safely inside her home, Kat placed the bag on her dresser to get a better look at the small creature. With those iridescent wings, maybe it was a type of dragonfly. It resembled an image from her childhood, perhaps a cartoon.... The creature gave a vigorous shake of its tail which emitted a sparkling array of dust. After that display, Kat just couldn't place where she'd seen such a specimen before. It stopped moving. Was it dead? When she caught it, it was in motion, but now...? Kat scrutinized the contents of the sandwich bag and wondered if more such creatures existed nearby. This one had been so easy to catch. Much easier than frogs. Yet, something about this specimen seemed familiar—its wings, its lean body—and she was just about to identify the species when it shook its tail again. Then, her thoughts dimmed.

On Kat's chest of drawers sat the vivarium that served as her science project. Hidden beneath river rocks and moss, a pump trickled water, a smaller version of the river. Tree bark lay scattered about with leaves and a few flies. She planned on adding several frogs since she enjoyed capturing them—it was a rush for her to pry open their mouths and discover if they had tongues or not. Some scientists recovered animals they had studied and tagged in previous years, but Kat only had to check their tongues to see if she had met them before. She marveled at how they managed to survive without them.

Two frogs existed in the vivarium now: one male and one female. The male kept Kat awake at night, singing, but she didn't mind much. She'd probably dissect him as soon as she received her grades. The school opted "to provide a humane education" that taught students to dissect through a computer program, but she liked the feel of frog flesh under her fingers.

Kat took the bag with the immobile creature, quickly crossed the room, swept open the lid of the vivarium, and dumped the unmoving creature inside. She thought she saw its wings twitch. It was enchanting. It practically sparkled.

Kat peered through the glass. She was concerned the life form wouldn't survive until the project was due. Already, the thing had changed colors. Its torso and limbs had turned a brownish green, the primary colors of her ecosystem. A delicate tail and wings had paled to echo the pink of Kat's bedroom walls.

Since the creature was so still and had been so easy to capture, Kat decided to inspect her hostage. After cautiously sliding the vivarium lid open and slipping her arm inside, she grabbed the specimen. It felt like a hundred velvet butterflies. Maybe it wouldn't die after all. Kat separated her cupped hands a bit and some sort of dust escaped, aimed toward her face, before she could again close her fingers.

Kat's nose tickled. She scratched it on her shoulder.

She peeked again, and more dust flew. Kat's nose didn't tickle this time. It danced the cha-cha. Nothing could have held back her sneeze. When she let go, her entire body went with it. She instinctively covered her mouth and nose with her hands, and when she brought them down, she discovered her newest acquisition had escaped.

"Ah, maaaaaan!" She wiped her hands on her shorts and stomped her foot. A titter rose from the carpet. Looking down, Kat saw a blob of brownish-green roll away from her shoe. The creature then stood and tried shaking itself dry to fly, but its wings were drenched from Kat's sneeze.

"Ooooh, g-ross!" Kat grabbed its legs with the tips of her fingers and lifted it into the air, dangling it before her face. Wings drooped, but it appeared to cross its arms in anger before again shaking its tail, covering itself and Kat's hand with a soft iridescence.

"Feisty, huh?"

"Kaaaaaat, dinner!" a voice called.

Kat placed the creature safely in her ecosystem. She wiped any magical goo from her hands and onto her shorts before closing the door behind her.

"I don't recall those shorts, Kat," her mom said. "They're *charming!*"

CHAPTER 3

Blaezi passed the last chunk of red clay that she recognized as home. Exiled? Exiled! She tripped with the thought, her wings sticking together with the heat. She reached down and touched a smooth bag attached at her waist by a sash of dried grass. Her Glamour. She had been allowed to take only three portion's worth. No Faye had ever before received such a harsh punishment. She moaned, jerked her wings apart, and ripped one. Sharp pain spread down the ribbons of her right wing and into her back. Tears the size of salt granules spilled from her eyes. "I don't even have any medicine!"

Ahead of her Thorne stopped. He withdrew butterfly salve from his pack and threw it at her—not *to* her, but *at* her.

She placed her hands on her hips. "You don't have to be such a snit, you know."

Thorne just kept flying, his strong wings carrying him.

"I didn't do anything to you!" She sniffled. "Why do you have to be so uppity?" Blaezi saw the muscles on his back twitch then tense, but he kept flying.

"Oh, right," she dug. "You're a *Natural*." Her face squinched as she said the last word. "You don't understand good manners." Thorne stopped flying but did not face her. Glad to have his attention, she spoke very slowly. "You... will put... the salve..." she held up the ointment, "...on my wing...." She wiggled her wing, then winced in pain. "Ooh.... Then we'll continue... after *you*..." she pointed at him, "tell *me*..." she touched her chest with the same fingertip, "...where we're going." With legs and arms crossed in defiance, she floated to the earth.

Thorne whirled, sending an explosion of magic she could not control. Her legs and arms sprung out in an "X" shape, and she soared toward him as fast as a gnat's sneeze until, just as quickly, she was thrust in a heap on the ground below him. Since their departure, Thorne had not spoken. Now, his voice, slow and strong, rumbled like the sound one hears when approaching a river.

"Good manners are all that keep me from silencing you. I came to your Council seeking help." He looked at her torn and wilting wing. "What they gave me instead was *you*."

Blaezi knew he was right to be disappointed. Her own People banished her until she could accomplish their tasks—with only three bags of Glamour—before the end of the second moon cycle. The single kindness they had extended to her was not telling Thorne she was an exile. She lifted herself from the heap his magic had thrown her into, raised her chin and looked him in the eyes, then resumed her attempt at applying the salve herself.

Thorne asked, "Why don't you use magic to do that?"

Tears burst forth and she sank into a bedraggled mess at his feet once more. "Because I only have three portions!"

"Oh, right. You Fayes remove your tails." He looked directly at her. "How do you conceal yourselves from humans?"

"Why would we want to do that?"

"So they see you only how and when you want them to." He squared his shoulders. "Don't you have a Moonbeam Ceremony?"

"Oh, *that*," Blaezi said. "Queen Tania demands it's performed immediately when a new Faye arrives."

Thorne nodded his approval.

"But I've never disguised myself on purpose." Blaezi shrugged. "What's the point?"

Thorne grunted and haphazardly threw enough Glamour her way to mend her wing as he turned around to continue on their journey. "You're slowing us down and we need to reach Rock River." This time, as Blaezi watched him streak ahead of her, she noticed a silver tuft beneath his large wings.

CHAPTER 4

As they entered Thorne's domain, Blaezi knew it was different. The earth was soft and dark, the color of the mortals' chocolate brownies. Its rich smell filled her nostrils. Little trees, not planted by man, sprouted voluntarily. Grass and wildflowers blew in the wind that didn't manage to blow quite as hard as at Blaezi's home. More animals scurried about because thick foliage provided more places for them to hide. Clear water rippled over river rocks, and fish were visible from shore. At Blaezi's home, waters ran red with mud.

The People here looked strange, too. Their wings and bodies revealed all the iridescence of a dewdrop, much different from home, where the sweltering temperatures this time of year turned the grass yellow and brittle so the Fayes wore yellow and red to blend with their surroundings. Here, the grass remained flush and green, and wildflowers of every color waved above it all. Flashes in shades Blaezi couldn't identify flitted past as Naturals went about their daily business. She'd never known so many green leaves.

Thorne hadn't spoken to her since he made the remark about removing tails. She wasn't sure what he'd meant, but as each Natural appeared to welcome him home, she understood more. Everywhere she saw a Natural, she saw a tail. Although Thorne's world differed from Blaezi's in many ways, the tails were the biggest shock of all. A myriad of shapes and sizes flounced past her to greet Thorne. Her eyes could not capture any pattern—curly, straight, long, feathery, short, spiky, mottled, shimmering—but all were original. Blaezi wondered what hers would look like if she were permitted to let it grow. To her knowledge, no Faye had ever been allowed to have a tail.

Blaezi longed to return home where she knew what to expect. A quick glance at the sun told her that if she were home, her shift would be over and she'd soon be dancing and eating with Dion and Diana. She struggled with the knowledge that unless she accomplished her tasks before the end of two moon cycles, she would never again be a Faye. She would be alone, a Solitary.

"T!" a large Natural swept from behind a tree and hugged Thorne. And to Blaezi's surprise, he hugged back.

"Dogwood! How you flying?"

The big guy chuckled and rubbed his belly. "Oh, you know me, T, a little low these days." Wearing a big grin, he looked at Blaezi several wing flaps behind and stopped. "Who's your friend?"

Blaezi, out of breath, caught up to them and waited to be introduced. Thorne didn't even pause before resuming flight. "She's not a friend. She's a Faye."

Dogwood's eyes grew large as he offered her a weak grin and pursued Thorne. Blaezi noticed Dogwood's tail separated into four sections of white dappled with brown.

Blaezi's mouth flew open. "Hey! He-ey! I'm a person. I have feelings. And you certainly shouldn't be acting so snitzy about Fayes when you came to *us* asking for help."

Dogwood turned to look at her. Thorne turned to look at him. Dogwood groaned. "T, you didn't."

"I did."

"And she volunteered to come by herself?"

Thorne looked at Blaezi a long while before saying, "Yeah, it was almost as if she had no choice."

At twilight, the Naturals bustled about preparing a feast. They entered the clearing from different directions carrying various treats. Some carried acorns, stored from last autumn, while others brought forth wild cherries. A plum floated on the glittering air as one Natural guided it in on Glamour. Laughter was thick as lightning bugs joined the celebration and hovered in a cluster above the forest floor, a glimmering chandelier for those below. A single note set the tone as a Natural began playing a flute. The hoots of nearby owls joined the song. Miniature versions of gourds Blaezi had seen in the Garden were covered with animal skins and Naturals drummed on them, calling to the heartbeat of the People. Here and there Naturals leapt to the glow of lightning bugs and danced in a ring.

Blaezi sat on a mushroom, to the side of the festivities, and watched the party. Thorne had been nearby at first, but had joined the dance with a Natural who winked at him. Blaezi watched as the girl's long, silver tail fluttered in harmony with the hummingbird feather fringe of her leather dress. She felt a pang of jealousy. Probably not because of the girl's luxurious tail, accompanying the whims of the wind. Definitely not because Thorne asked the girl and her tail to dance, either. No, certainly not.

No one asked Blaezi to dance, but they knew she was there. They stared at her. They whispered about her.

"I hear she's a Faye."

"Not much to look at without a tail."

Whoo. Whoo. The owls called.

"Can she really help us?"

"Thorne doesn't make mistakes, but she might be his first."

"Let's give her a chance. She might be our answer."

Whoo. Whoo.

"The Fayes must not be much fun. She's not dancing or anything."

After the last comment, Blaezi's throat constricted and ached up through her nose. She wanted to go home. Dion, or some other Faye, would have asked her to dance many times, and she would have glided above the forest floor with the rest of them. Diana would have danced with countless Fayes and fallen in love with each of them. At home everyone would gossip about last night's Midsummer Festival. Their words might include her exile or they could have already forgotten about her. Tonight was to be a continuation of Midsummer fun, with Diana and Dion scheduled to compete in a magic contest. She'd helped them both prepare. They were probably competing now. She imagined her friends playing without her there to cheer them.

Then she realized they might not be having fun at all. They might be battling grubs without the skills to do so. Or they might be hungry. And it was her fault. She had to think of some way to save them.

Blaezi opened her eyes wide and pretended to look at the stars, forcing back her tears. Twinkling brightness blurred her vision, and the tears disappeared. Distracted, she leaned back, rested her head on a stone, and stared.

She had never seen so many stars. How could she not have noticed them all? Perhaps the lights from the human cities made the stars seem fewer. Tonight, however, no major human dwellings lay nearby. Wispy strands of clouds stretched like spider webs across the sky. For the first time since her exile, she felt a twinge of excitement.

"Glamorous, isn't it?" a voice beside her whispered.

No one had spoken to Blaezi since her arrival. The voice startled her, but she wouldn't, or couldn't, stop looking at the sky.

She nodded instead.

"I wouldn't think you'd be interested in simple things," said the voice.

The tightening of her throat returned, but the tears did not. She found her tongue and said, "Why not?" She allowed her gaze to glimpse her companion and saw it was Thorne. "How can something so beautiful be simple?"

Thorne's voice lost its comforting resonance. "Oh, that's the sort of thinking I expected from you." He got up and Blaezi felt her body lifting against her will as Thorne used his magic to move her to a flying position. "C'mon. It's time to introduce you and tell everyone why you're here. If you know what is good for you, you'll let me do the talking. Just keep your pretty little Faye mouth shut." He flittered off.

Pretty? "Did you just call me pretty?" Blaezi called. He was gone, though, so she examined his wings and back and tail for the umpteenth time that day.

Thorne darted back to her side and scowled. "Well, what are you waiting for? Will you follow me, or do I have to move you myself?"

"Ughssz!" Blaezi said. "You're such a hummingbird." She fluttered her wings. "I was just thinking that, of course, my mouth is pretty." She grinned. "It's mine. I was merely surprised you noticed."

As Thorne rolled his eyes, she flew past him to the middle of the ring. When he caught her, he whispered, "Figure of speech. Remember what I meant, but you don't have to remember what I said." Then he turned to the noisy crowd. "Friends, I have an introduction to make."

The flute stopped. The dancing halted. All Naturals looked at Blaezi, the atmosphere similar to the previous evening.

Why did People always interrupt fun to humiliate her? What would this group do? The People's tortures were horrible because few things killed or even weakened them, so pain could last forever. Her memory recalled ancient stories concerning fire ants, and she shuddered. She was already exiled. What would the Naturals do when they discovered her fate?

Thorne grabbed Blaezi's hand and pulled her closer. "As many of you suspect, she is a Faye."

The crowd looked at each other with furrowed expressions. A few booed and the owls called. *Whooo? Whooo?*

Thorne laughed, "Yet, you'll all want to know her name because she's going to help us. Blaezi is going to blaze a trail to help us connect with the humans."

"Wha...?!" Blaezi asked in unison with the crowd. Thorne twisted her hand and she winced.

"As you all know," Thorne continued, "the humans are moving in on our forest. More dwellings appear with each moon. Soon, our forest may disappear altogether."

The Naturals nodded and murmured their discontent.

"I went to the Faye Council to ask for help, and they offered us Blaezi."

A Natural on the front row shook his finger at Thorne. "How dare you."

"He cares nothing about our history with them!" cried another.

"Silence!" bellowed Thorne. Blaezi relaxed. Finally— something familiar. She was much more accustomed to his angry voice than the cordial one he'd used during the rest of this speech. "How dare I *not* try to help my fellow People? Our way of life is coming to an end. We all see it. We need help. You should recognize that I, of all Naturals, remember our history with them.

But we have no other choice." He paused then and looked across the Naturals to one sitting outside the circle. "If you don't believe me, ask Raine."

All eyes moved to the old man nodding apart from the rest. His wings barely moved as he flew to stand beside Thorne and Blaezi. He touched Blaezi's chin and raised it to study her eyes. Blaezi hadn't realized she was shivering until his warm fingers calmed her to stillness. Then he examined her wings. "Yes," the old one said. "Yes, this little one will help us." He spoke to the crowd. "Danger is near. She may be our only hope."

"What do you mean danger is near?" Blaezi asked. "That's what my reader told me at the Midsummer Festival. 'Danger is near you,' she said, 'and trouble will be your guide, salvation, and destiny.'"

The old man smiled. Thorne dropped her hand and stepped back.

She gripped the ancient hand with both of hers. "What did she mean by that? What do *you* mean?" She turned to Thorne and pinched him. "Tell me why I'm here. What am I expected to do? I'm just a Garden Guard!"

Out of the corner of his mouth, Thorne said, "And from what I hear, you're as good at that job as you are at keeping your mouth shut."

"What's a Garden Guard?" asked one of the group.

"Yeah," cried another, "if she doesn't think she can handle it...."

Raine held up his hands. "A Garden Guard is a very important position in the Faye world. Blaezi will explain her duty."

Blaezi tugged her ear. "Well," she glanced at Thorne, "in the *simplest* terms... I guard humans' gardens."

The crowd gasped.

With wide eyes, a little boy asked, "Do you fight?"

"Uh... yeah." Blaezi appreciated this admiration. "It's a dirty job, but, uh, some Faye has to do it."

Dogwood said, "So you're accustomed to danger. What do you fight? What is it that you guard against?"

"Oh... against attack by pests."

A breeze ruffled her wings.

"Pests like us?" sneered a rough looking Natural in the back.

"Rock," Raine said, "you know that's not true." He pursed his lips. "Or you *would* know if you had paid more attention to the People's lore. She guards their food, and she's going to help us learn to cohabitate with the humans. Isn't that correct, Thorne?"

"Yes. I brought her here because the Fayes know the ways of the humans—unlike us—and have lived with them for hundreds of summers. Blaezi has offered to teach us to survive with a smaller forest and more human interaction." He pierced Blaezi with eyes that dared her to deny his statement.

She offered the crowd a grin and a shrug. "Sure," she said. "No wind off my wings."

CHAPTER 5

The sun shining through the windows might have awakened Kat if she weren't already dressed and staring at the sleeping creature in her vivarium. It had burrowed between a rock and a branch placed there to represent a tree. Although it had appeared pink last night, this morning the creature's body, wings, and tail seemed to be the same pale green as the leaves surrounding it. This color would definitely show up against her carpet and walls if she managed to sneeze and somehow drop it again. Of course, this wouldn't happen.

She walked over to a vase of pink, artificial roses and yanked them out, then reached in with her other hand. From the bottom of the vase, she removed the Styrofoam frog that had held the flowers in place. She replaced the flowers, and with the green squishy square in her hand, Kat turned toward her dressing table, a white table with gold trim and a cushioned stool pulled beneath it. Tiny pink petals and polka dots covered the surface of the cushion. It was the same fabric as her comforter, curtains, and lampshade. On the table's surface lay an assortment of neatly organized beauty aids. Inside a delicately tooled iron cup, a glass held an assortment of makeup brushes. A matching case, set on the other side, held makeup. A coordinating tray held perfume and lotions. Kat pulled a tissue from a box reflecting the same tooling as everything else and spread it flat on the table. She lay the flower frog on top and put another tissue on it to resemble a top sheet on a miniature lumpy mattress. From a drawer she retrieved four bobby pins and set them on the table. Everything she needed for her research was in place.

The mirror reflected two concentration lines between her eyebrows. Too young to have wrinkles, but old enough to realize she should prevent them, she took a long breath and exhaled, willing calmness to her features. When the creases disappeared, she smiled. One could never practice a smile too much. Wrinkles around the mouth could easily be smoothed with plastic surgery. Meanwhile, boys liked girls who smiled, and girls always looked prettier with dazzling teeth. She grabbed another tissue as she removed her teeth whitening devices. Then she smeared the residual gel still clinging to her teeth onto the tissue.

Kat returned to the vivarium and removed the creature. The activity inside her hands indicated it was awake but wasn't as strong as it had been.

"I bet you're not eating, little lady, are you? You must be hungry." She paused. "Hmmm. . . Let's see. I've given you frog food and fish food. I guess you don't like either." She placed the creature flat on the little bed she had made with the foam flower frog and tissues and held it captive with one hand. Its tail wiggled. "It wouldn't do for you to get sick and die before my project is due." Cupping her hand so as not to smash the creature, Kat moved her fingers to spread its legs. "I haven't even classified you yet." With her other hand she grabbed a bobby pin and pushed it efficiently through the tissue, securing one of the legs. "We should be able to take care of that today." She stuck another bobby pin around the other leg. Sensing the futility, the creature stopped its weak attempts to escape and lay still. "We'll get you food in no time."

"Kaaaaaaat!"

She plunked in another bobby pin.

"Kat!"

She placed the fourth and final bobby pin with satisfaction.

Her bedroom door swung open.

"Kat," her father said, "couldn't you hear me calling?"

Kat charmed him with a smile. "I'm sorry, Dad. I wasn't thinking."

Her father's reprimand melted. "Princess, you're *always* thinking."

Some of the creature's sparkling dander had transferred to her hands. Kat ran fingers through her hair and leaned nonchalantly against the dressing table, hiding the work-in-progress from her father's line of sight. "I was just trying to put my face on for school. I'm having major breakouts."

"Well, you know you always look pretty to me, but I'm partial." He looked at his watch. "I need to take you to class early today. Glad you're a morning person! Most teenagers are still in bed." He smiled at his daughter. "You ready?"

"Um. Yeah, I'll just be a sec," Kat said, a smile hiding her annoyance at leaving a project unfinished.

"You certainly look ready." Her father cocked his head. "I don't know what you've done to your hair this morning, but you could be in a shampoo commercial."

As her father left, Kat called after him, "I'll meet you in the car!" Then she turned to her creature. "I'll see you this afternoon."

CHAPTER 6

The rich earth was cool against Blaezi's skin as she rolled over to sleep just a bit longer. Inhaling its thick scent, she snuggled into the fallen log that offered protection from the sun. Honeysuckle wafted in on a breeze and provoked her tummy to growl. Hoping the yumsies would have food gathered and ready, she stretched and yawned, then blinked several times at her surroundings.

The memories of the last two days returned. The survival of two bands of People had suddenly become her responsibility. She just wanted to go home, but she couldn't do that until she helped the Naturals. Her stomach growled again. No yumsies would greet her with leaf-covered bark piled high with such delicacies as jelly beans and okra. At least she didn't think so. She flew out of the log and shook the blanket of dirt from her body.

The forest seemed empty. The leaves rustled and birds sang, but no one appeared to inhabit the thicket at all. "Naturals," she muttered with a snort. "They must be so lazy they're still asleep."

They certainly hadn't prepared food. Half hoping to see the others and half hoping to avoid them, Blaezi followed her nose to the area where trumpet-shaped yellow-white flowers with slim yellow tongues popped their heads out of a lush cascading green mass. Here and there, Naturals fluttered their wings while poking their heads into the flowers, feasting.

Apprehensive, she flew over. "Hi! Mind if I join you?"

"Corf nah," replied a plump body with its mouth full. When he pulled his head from the flower, she saw the garbled voice belonged to Dogwood. He swallowed. "What I meant to say was 'of course not.' We don't have any rules about eating here. C'mon!" He waved Blaezi over. "We'll show you the finer techniques of drinking nectar."

Blaezi then noticed they had been playing a game. Without using wings, several leapt onto separate bumblebees, feet first. Attempting to balance, they bent their knees and held out their arms. Blaezi thought the sport looked like the human children of the Garden skateboarding. Except of course the obvious. Humans never boarded a buzzing, flying, irritated bumblebee.

"The one who drains a flower first wins," explained Dogwood just as a lanky Natural fell. "Watch him," said Dogwood. "That's Laurel. He's always doing something fun. Pretty soon, others will be over there imitating him." Laurel's hair was the same shade as the honeysuckle petals, and he appeared to be all arms, legs, and gangly wings. He managed to catch himself and attempted to flit away before the bee went after him. Unfortunately for him, the bee was faster. "Oooh," winced Dogwood. "That's gotta hurt. As you just noticed, not all make it to suckle." They watched as the injured Natural spit in the dirt and jumped around holding his bottom. "I'll be back. He'll need some help to make mud paste."

She waved goodbye and shifted her attention to the others still on their bees and drinking nectar. The bees flew beneath the flowers, and the players' tails looked vaguely familiar hanging out of the petals. One in particular caught her attention, especially since she had studied its silver tuft—it was Thorne's. The tail beside Thorne's certainly must be the reason that Fayes removed them. An assortment of gray, black, and brown jumbled in a strangled mass. Each dismal strand seemed to be a different length, making this tail the least aesthetic Blaezi had seen. The tail lacked the soft whimsy of the others, too. It looked as hard as stone. As Blaezi contemplated just how the tail might be able to get any uglier, it and Thorne's tail began to wiggle as each Natural squirmed his way out of the mouth of the flower to declare himself the winner. Holding up their arms and jumping into full flight, they exclaimed at almost the exact same time, "Full!" The ugly tail belonged to Rock, the one who had accused her of calling them pests.

Blaezi thought his tail matched his attitude.

The others peeked around the foliage to see who had won. Dogwood and the fallen Natural, who now sported a mud pack on his rump, congratulated the winner. Thorne and Rock disagreed about who should celebrate, though. Rock looked down his round, crooked nose at Thorne. "It's plain and simple that I won. I usually do."

Thorne laughed, but it was one of those laughs that startled the birds into their nests.

With mud still on his hands, Dogwood squeezed his head between them. "Now do you really want to argue about this when the sun is so hot?" He twisted his head to look at both of them, his eyes open in a silly way. Fanning himself, he flung mud in Rock's face. Thorne grinned as Dogwood continued, "Why don't we join the others for a swim?"

Blaezi chimed in, "Or we can play a different game if you're still hungry." They looked at her as if they'd forgotten she existed. "Um," she scratched her ear. "Yeah, there's this one game we played all the time back home." She couldn't stop her words. Rock wiped the mud on his face and managed to smear it more. "If the yumsies didn't have food ready yet, we'd play games with honeysuckle, too." They looked interested. Apparently, everyone liked games.

"What's a yumsy?" Dogwood asked.

But Blaezi was still talking. "See, we'd all line up and try to drink as many flowers as possible as fast as possible." Thorne and Dogwood cocked their heads, but Rock just raised his eyebrows. "I know. I know. No beeboarding," she said, "but it's really fun."

Beeboarding? mouthed Rock with mock astonishment.

Blaezi ignored him. She was gaining confidence. "Sometimes there was so much that you feel sick and can't eat anything the next day either. I was pretty good at it. Do you guys want to play?"

The others gathered around Thorne, Rock, and Dogwood. They all stared at her.

"Of course, if you don't want...."

Rock sneered. "That's a typical game for a Faye."

"Why? Because it's good? Because it's fun?" Blaezi's hands were on her hips and she was getting angry now. The bag of Glamour tempted her fingers as she touched it. One of her allotments could teach Rock a lesson, but she decided he wasn't worth it. "You're such a drought on fun that you alone probably gave Naturals a bad name."

"Oh?" Rock slung his arms around the necks of a couple of players who had the misfortune of standing nearby. "We have a bad name? Says who?" The Naturals beneath his arms looked uncomfortable to be in such close proximity with Rock, but gave Blaezi, not Rock, the look that meant they wanted *her* to disappear.

"All I know," she looked with what she hoped was a winning smile at the two struggling beneath Rock's arms, "is that *some* Naturals have a bad reputation."

"You don't know anything," Rock glared at her. Then he squeezed his new buddies so hard their eyes bulged and their wings sprung straight out. "All right, Dogwood, these Naturals want to go swimming!"

"I think I'll stay here," said Thorne. "I'm going to eat a bite more and then catch up."

"Don't bother," called Rock. "You're nothing but trouble anyway. Both of you. I'm not surprised you went and got yourself a Faye."

Only Dogwood lingered. "Don't worry about it, T. Brush it off, Blaezi. He's just a grumpy ditzlesnit."

"He's a grub." Blaezi gritted her teeth and seethed. "And I'm not stupid. I do know stuff."

"Really?" asked Thorne.

"Yeah, really."

"Then do you know why none of us will be playing your game?"

"None of you?" Blaezi frowned. "I thought only Rock didn't like it."

"No," Dogwood shook his head. "Naturals don't play games like that."

Thorne shoved past to pick up an acorn and crack it. "We don't waste food here. We use only what we need so we'll always have plenty."

Blaezi thrust her wings back. "But you all raced to eat the honeysuckle."

"Only as much as we needed," said Dogwood as he placed a hand on her shoulder. "Also, it helps them grow. We help the bees do double-duty in fertilizing the flowers—without sucking them all dry at once."

"*We* don't have a Garden for backup food," muttered Thorne as he dipped his hand in the acorn for more meat.

Blaezi wanted to cry again. She'd never thought of it like that. At home, food was always available in one form or another.

Unfortunately, that would be different this summer with the Garden closed. Maybe she didn't know so much after all.

Dogwood spoke up, "Blaezi, do you know where we come from?"

"Everyone knows that." She glanced at Thorne who seemed more interested in the food on his face than her recitation of the story she'd learned many summers ago:

> It only happens when the moon is bright,
> and two People in love kiss good night.
> If they kiss 'neath a moonbeam's glow,
> a new one will slide down and giggle hello.

"See! You do know something after all!" Dogwood patted her cheek. "And I'll tell you something else," he whispered.

Blaezi leaned in, eager to conspire.

"Rock came down head first on the moonbeam and landed hard. That's why he's so mean."

Blaezi laughed and it felt good. When Thorne started laughing, she knew he'd been listening all along. She was glad he knew that she knew *something*.

Dogwood said, "He feels a little threatened any time someone invades our territory." He chuckled. "A long time ago, he even cursed humans."

Blaezi's mouth flew open. "Cursed?" She shook her head. "That's forbidden!"

Thorne's mouth formed a grim line. "Maybe for Fayes—but not for Naturals. It's not something we like to do, but we know it's sometimes required for protection." He raised an eyebrow in response to her condemning frown. "Fayes once did it, too." His eyes slowly scanned Blaezi's body. "Your queen has reasons for making her People forget."

Blaezi raised her chin. "I'm sure she does."

"And," Dogwood said, "Rock's just being himself. He's still a Natural, so he can't be all bad."

"Just ignore most of what he says," Thorne added.

Dogwood turned to go and said, "And we're grateful that you plan to help us."

"No problem." Blaezi touched her fingers to her lips. "I'm full of ideas."

Dogwood flew toward the injured player who had fallen behind the others. He slung the Natural's arm over his shoulder. Together they flew out of sight.

"Full of mushroom soil is more like it," said Thorne.

She turned to him. "And what's this about you 'getting yourself a Faye'? I'm not your property."

"That's not what he meant," Thorne retorted.

Blaezi didn't ask what he *had* meant because she was tired of showing how much she didn't know.

"Well," she looked away and sighed, "just so you didn't go getting the wrong idea."

CHAPTER 7

Blaezi followed Thorne as he returned to the honeysuckle. After she had her fill—and no more—she looked around for him. Eyes closed, he rested on a bundle of honeysuckle growing along the ground. She slid beside him.

He glanced at her and then closed his eyes again. "You were exiled, weren't you?"

Blaezi was in motion. "I think I'm going to get more honeysuckle."

"No, you're not." His magic was strong. She was quickly back in the reclined position. "What were your terms? All Fayes and Naturals know Queen Tania offers impossible terms to taunt her exiles. If you can meet the terms, you may return home. Of course, no Faye has ever succeeded. Our People can't live alone or they'll die. You're just lucky I came along to offer another troupe of People to exist with."

Blaezi couldn't move. Not because he was holding her with his magic but because she was scared.

"Don't worry," Thorne said. "I'm not going to tell. The Naturals would be angrier with me than with you. They don't want a Faye reject."

Now that her reason to fear was dismissed, she was offended. "I'm not a reject!"

"Yes. You are." He opened his eyes and looked at her. "What

do you think it is to be exiled? They get rid of you. They say you can't come home anymore. You'll never be able to see your friends again. Unless they seek to find you, which is unlikely if you've been exiled." He closed his eyes again. "When you're exiled, you have no friends and no home. You're a discard. Nobody wants you."

Blaezi hadn't thought of that. Surely her friends missed her. Would anyone try to find her? Could they try to help her? It had been several nights since the Midsummer Festival. Maybe they'd find her soon—if they even wanted to.

"Well, I wasn't completely exiled, was I?" Blaezi countered. "I was sent with you. They must not have wanted to get rid of me." She didn't mention the Fayes viewed her appointment to the Naturals as worse than exile—and much more amusing.

Thorne looked at her. "Have you been sniffing pixie dust? You're in trouble. Rock was right about that. You are trouble." He looked at his hands. "So, tell me your terms so I can help."

"You'd help me?" Blaezi was flattered and her wings fluttered.

"I'll help you," Thorne said. "The sooner we meet your terms, the sooner you're away from me."

"Away from you? I thought you wanted me to help you. Ahh...." Blaezi moved a little closer to Thorne. "Why? Do I make you nervous?"

He leaned so close that she felt his body heat. He placed fists on either side of her body, crushing the honeysuckle bloom where she sat. She felt no escape. "Really nervous." He grinned at her and leaned back again. She released a long breath she hadn't realized she held. He continued, "The longer you're here, the more the risk I'll get discovered for bringing an exiled Faye. Naturals don't like me asking the Fayes for help."

Blaezi's wings drooped. "If the Fayes are so horrible, why did they even send me, as useless as you seem to think I am, to help you learn how to cope with the humans?"

"They owe me."

"Ha!" cried Blaezi. "Since when are Fayes indebted to Naturals?"

"Rock is right about another thing, too." Thorne stood up. "You don't know anything."

CHAPTER 8

The sound of water over rocks rushed toward Blaezi. She knew the sounds. Back home the Garden held several fountains and ponds, and in the small wood flowed a rivulet of water the Fayes called the River, but it didn't sound quite like this. She'd never heard water so loud. When she flew within view, she knew the River didn't look like this either. These banks were so wide a fallen tree couldn't cross.

She flew toward the Naturals who were swimming and flying about the water's edge. Some bathed while others tormented the fish and dragonflies.

Never one to be left out, Blaezi decided to give this new river a try. Slipping her foot in the water, she realized too late that the current was strong. It tugged her in foot first and encircled her, pulling her deeper and deeper. Before she could call for help, her head went under. She hit a rock and somehow flew up long enough to gasp for breath. She tried to fly away, but her wings were drenched, and she couldn't shake them dry. The weight of water thrust her down again. A tree branch scratched as she was forced under it. She reached for her Glamour, her precious three bags of Glamour. If there were ever a time to use one, it was now. But they were gone. Desperate, she screamed and water filled her mouth.

The People weren't meant to die. They could live forever if they wanted to. All they needed was food, water, shelter, light, nature, and other People. She, at least, wanted to live a little while longer. She'd planned on going to the Glamour Fields instead of dying, but now she just wanted to live long enough to have someone miss her when she was gone.

With a thunk, her body fell on something hard, and she felt herself surfacing, almost floating. It was not as smooth as flight, but she somehow swooshed through the water with the same jerking movements of a Faye first testing her wings—swoosh forward, then back, swoosh forward, then back. As if she were riding on some big wing being lifted from the water and into the sky. This rescue-wing wasn't soaring, though, it was flapping. Her chest hurt as she coughed. Once she was able to fill her body with air, she realized what had saved her.

She looked at its hard shell and bright streak down one cheek as it swam upriver to where the others played. The red-eared turtle must have been sunning on the tree limb her body slammed against. Recognizing safety, Blaezi relaxed and tried to hug the turtle, but the shell was too hard and she was too weak. Instead, she breathed in relief and let the sun dry her wings. After the rush of excitement from knowing her life was saved came the realization she would never be able to accomplish her terms of exile: Her Glamour was gone. When the turtle swam onto shore, a tear-wracked Blaezi met the group of Naturals.

"I'll never get home.... It's gone!" she babbled from atop the turtle's large shell.

Rock laughed and returned to his game of tag with a horsefly.

The others worried. "How is she going to help us now that her mind was lost in the river?"

Dogwood arrived with a leafy substance, fed it to the turtle and petted its nose. Blaezi cried and made no move to fly down.

Thorne stepped forward and patted the shell. *Bthum-Bthum-*

Bthum. "Thanks for bringing her back to us. We don't know what we'd do without her."

Blaezi continued to cry. "What'll I do?"

Thorne seemed to ignore all the Naturals watching him and gossiping about Blaezi. Instead, he calmed their fears by calling to Blaezi, "Now that you've had your swim, why don't you climb on down and tell us all about it?"

Blaezi just sobbed harder and threw herself, face down, onto the turtle's shell.

"Ha," said Thorne, pretending to laugh as he turned to the crowd. "She's been teaching me this new game. You know how those Fayes are." The blank eyes meeting his informed him that, no, they did not. He turned around to her and called, "Ready or not, here I come!" before sweeping her into his arms and swooping off into the forest. Thorne deposited her on a moss-covered rock as she continued to sniffle. He flew away a few paces and crossed his arms. He started to say something, paused, and flew a little ways farther. When he returned this time, he spoke and had difficulty controlling his volume. He didn't want to speak too loudly for fear someone might be listening.

"I don't know how or why, but your Glamour is not as strong as ours. That's why you couldn't fight the current."

She sobbed harder. He continued, "Maybe you'll have stronger Glamour when you— "

"Stronger?" Blaezi asked. "There won't be any*more!*"

Thorne crossed his arms. "What are you gibbering about?"

"They're gone!" Her shoulders slumped. "All gone. I just wanted to swim and now they're gone and I'll never get home!" A nearby deer flipped its white tail and ran off.

He flew close and grabbed her arm. "Shhh! Shhh." She cried harder so he gave her arm a shake. "Shhhh. There's no need to yell.

Do you want to get us both exiled?"

She collapsed, embracing him with her tiny, wet arms. She sobbed into his chest until he patted her back.

"OUCH!" She jerked from his arms and tried to rub her back. "What?!" she shrieked. "Are you trying to beat me to death since I only *nearly* drowned? Are you trying to find out just how immortal I am? I may be a Faye, but I'm one of the People same as you, so stop trying to kill me!"

"I didn't know how hard to pat," Thorne said and tried to withdraw, but Blaezi stayed close. "I thought you were tougher than that."

Her face crumpled into tears again, "I don't have any way to defend myself. It's gone.... All gone." Then she was back against him, her body shaking with sobs as she suspected he calculated how long it would take to sun himself in order to rid his body of her tears and the river's water.

When her sobs subsided, he was as wet as she, but he wasn't sure if she was finished crying or just taking a breath. He took his chance—careful not to pat her on the back. "So... Blaezi... do you want to tell me what happened?" He waited.

Finally, she sat up and wiped her nose with his wing. "I've been trying to tell you."

Thorne wanted to finish the job the river had started, but calmly said, "I'm sorry. I didn't understand. Would you try again... please?"

Offering a weak smile, she said, "I went to the water because I thought I could find you. But when I got there, the water looked so cool and so much bigger than the River back home," at the word *home*, her face contorted and Thorne thought she would start crying again, but she continued, "and I hadn't been for a swim in a while...."

"Go on."

"I figured I could swim before talking to you about my terms."

"You came to the river to tell me?" His wings perked up.

"Yes," she sniffled. "But now it's no use!" She almost collapsed again, but he caught her elbows and pushed her upright. The surprise registered on her face and stopped her tears.

"Why is it 'no use'?"

"Because... because... *because* I've lost my Glamour!" she splurted.

Thorne dropped her elbows and stood over her. "Is that all?"

She blinked up at him.

"Is *that* all you're skitting out about?"

"I'll never meet my terms now unless I get help. Lots of help." She smiled her crooked smile at him. "You want to help a Faye in distress?"

"No," he said. "But I want to help *me*. The sooner we can exchange information and help, the sooner you'll be gone."

"Now, now, that's not true." Blaezi smiled and fluttered her wings. "You told the turtle you didn't know what you'd do without me."

"I thought you'd gone crazy or, at the least, become hysterical."

Patting the rock where he had been sitting, she said, "I'll do anything you want me to if you just help me get home."

He raised an eyebrow. "Anything?"

"Almost anything." She sighed and looked toward the river. The splashing and giggling of the Naturals floated through the afternoon. "Your river's not like back home," she said.

He had just been thinking he might tolerate her. "Well, we're proud of what we have, as lacking in show as it may be. We think it's glamorous in its own way." He glared at her. "It took control of you, didn't it?" She would provide a lot of laughs, the way she appeared like Queen Tania herself, riding in, soaked to the core, on a turtle's back.

"Oh. I agree." Blaezi didn't want to make him mad again. She should save that for special occasions so she could enjoy it more. "I mean this is so much bigger than ours back home. Ours is slow and pretty quiet. In the late summer it dwindles to a trickle until a mosquito could walk across the river bed."

"Are you sure it's a river? It sounds like a creek to me."

"What's a creek?"

He was astounded at her lack of knowledge of the natural world. "Oh, it's 'slow and pretty quiet' and 'in the late summer, it dwindles to a trickle...'."

Blaezi tugged on her ear. "You're making fun of me."

"Yep."

"I guess I'll let you—just once."

Thorne leaned back and cupped his head in his hands. "I'll show you a creek sometime, and you tell me if it's like your River."

"Okay."

"There's one condition, though."

"Oh," Blaezi grinned at him, "what's that?"

Thorne levitated above the rock. "Tell me your terms."

"Fine." She tried imitating him, realizing too late that her wings were still heavy with water. "But not until you take me to the creek."

CHAPTER 9

Kat walked into her room with an afternoon snack. She refused to eat refreshments from a paper towel. Likewise, she wouldn't drink from plastic cups. So chocolate chip cookies occupied the center of her mom's good china, and cold milk filled a glass. The treats looked prettier this way. When things are pretty, everything is much nicer.

After placing the snack on her nightstand, she plopped on the bed beside her backpack. From the bag she pulled a stack of library books. Setting aside *The Prairie Plains* and *Water Critters*, she reached for a chocolate chip cookie and her most likely source: *Creatures of the Ozark Plateau*. She had eaten her third cookie, and looked through at least that many books, when she realized none of the photographs remotely resembled what she had pinioned on her dressing table. Perhaps she needed another, closer look. She stacked the books beside her bed and whisked the crumbs from lap and comforter before depositing them in the trashcan. She grabbed one last cookie and sauntered over to her dressing table.

But the creature was gone!

The bobby pins were in place and the tissue hadn't moved much, although it looked a little bunched up in the middle. Leaning closer, Kat took another bite of cookie. A few crumbs fell on the tissue and the bunched up part of the tissue moved. The specimen had transformed to the same color as the tissue. Kat moved her face very close to the twitching mound of white and saw the creature was there but had completely faded to white. She gasped. "It's a chameleon!"

Kat rushed to her laptop and typed *chameleon* into the search engine. She clicked on one site after another. Green and scaly lizards stuck their tongues out at her. "Ew. Those don't look like what I caught at all." Still, she clicked on the link to chameleon food. "A variety of insects supply the healthiest diet for your growing chameleon," the article stated. "If you catch your own wild insects, remember brightly colored bugs are often considered lethal in the animal kingdom. Opt for crickets, cicadas, grasshoppers, etc." Kat knew her creature wouldn't eat insects. She'd already tried. She made a mental note that after she received her perfect score on her ecosystem she should experiment with the frogs, though. Perhaps she'd give them some colorful food... lady bugs maybe.

She hadn't given up on her query yet. Her creature did change colors to mimic its environment, after all. It just might be a chameleon. She clicked another page on health hazards. Chameleons required plenty of water and sunlight or they became sick. "Easy," she said aloud. Chameleons were skilled at hiding illness, but one sign they were sick was if they stopped eating. "That's it!" Kat researched further and discovered holding them against their will makes them nervous and suicidal. Go figure. It seemed a lot of things made chameleons nervous. Being around other chameleons for instance. Not only was she not supposed to cage it with another chameleon, but also she should keep it in something without reflective surfaces—like vivariums—or it would freak out.

"That's weird." She looked over at the creature, motionless, on her dressing table. "I caught you because you were looking at yourself in my mirror. And you seemed to like what you saw."

She studied the captive's arms, legs, wings, and tail. "Funny," she said, "you don't look like a lizard. You look like a—" The creature wiggled a little, emitting its sparkly dander, and Kat shook her head. On second thought, maybe it did. She caught her reflection and tossed her head so her hair fell into place, before returning to the spiky, wart covered bodies on her screen. "Listen, I'd be happy, too, if I looked so much better than everyone else!" She laughed then typed in another search: *chameleons with wings*.

Nothing useful appeared. The reason "wings" and "chameleons" even popped up together was because of the winged insects chameleons enjoyed. At least all but Kat's chameleon enjoyed. She also found many sites on dragons, fairies and other fantastical creatures. Kat examined some of the drawings and descriptions and then glanced at her capture, which wiggled again. Kat felt a strange sensation. "Stupid. There's no such thing as fairies. I'm so not reading that." Kat closed her screen. "Like I'm one of those kids who sits around reading fantasy novels and pretending the creatures are real." She placed her laptop on the back corner of her desk, making sure to leave the desk tidy.

She returned to her captive. "Now, what am I going to do with you if you won't eat? I can't have a dead chameleon in my project."

She looked closer. All but one of the cookie crumbs was gone from the table. The one that had not disappeared seemed to be bouncing—or was it levitating? "So that's it," Kat whispered. With each movement of the tissue-white creature, the crumb moved a little closer toward the creature's mouth. "You like chocolate, too, huh?"

CHAPTER 10

Each night, it seemed to Blaezi, was Midsummer Festival with the Naturals. If she didn't watch herself, she might grow to like their ways—at least some of them.

The Naturals had been kinder to her today. Blaezi wondered if their lack of animosity was due to her escapades at the river or if they believed she could help. No matter what, something seemed to have made them forgive, a little, that she was a Faye.

Thorne led Blaezi deep into the woods until they heard the faint tinkle of water. She recognized the sound. The River. The Faye River! She followed him to the edge and soaked up the sight. It looked familiar. Although not the same, it reminded her of home.

"Is this like your River?" asked Thorne. Blaezi nodded.

"Are you disappointed that it's only a creek?"

Her eyes snapped at him. "Why would I be? Just because it's different doesn't make yours better."

The heat of late evening met the humidity of dawn, and Thorne crouched to dip his tail in the water's coolness. "I'm surprised you said that."

"Why?"

Thorne said, "You don't know where creeks come from, do you?"

Blaezi felt lured to a trap. She whispered, "No."

"Well, if you follow this creek," he pointed the direction of a rising sun, "you'll get to the river—the real one. The Natural one." He continued. "And if you follow the creek that way," he pointed the direction of a setting moon, "you'll find your home."

No wonder Blaezi felt connected to this place. "You mean this creek is the same as mine?"

"Umhmm."

"And this creek flows into your river?"

"Umhmm."

"And that's why the current's not as strong by the time it reaches home?"

"Just like your Glamour. It's from a simple source."

"Glamour?" She turned on him. "Fayes are strong and we don't get our Glamour from *Naturals*." She said the word as if she'd bitten into a bitter pecan. "We're not the same. Don't even try to act like Fayes ever received anything from Naturals. We're nothing like you."

"No," he bowed his head, "you certainly aren't, or you'd know more." Thorne appeared to speak to the grass along the creek. "You probably don't even know what I'm talking about." He stood before Blaezi could comment. "Remember though, it's like you said, just because we're different doesn't make you better. We're more alike than you think." He flew a distance along the creek and paused to look over his shoulder. "When you calm down, I'll be back. We need to discuss your terms."

Blaezi's anger went clear to her toes, but she couldn't hate him tonight. He'd brought her here. In a way, it was like coming home. She inhaled deeply and looked at the last of the evening's stars. There weren't as many as there were with the Naturals, just like at home.

She peered across the creek bed and through the leaves. In

the distance she saw many bright stars close to the ground. They were so familiar. Some moved in pairs like shooting stars, hovering above paths, casting long beams and then disappearing into the night. Some went out and came on in a different nearby place. Blaezi sat on the bank and dipped her feet in the water, watching the ripples as she wiggled her toes. She listened to the ordinary forest sounds of fish jumping, insects chirping, and owls hooting combined with dogs barking and doors—was that what they called them?—slamming.

After a while, Thorne returned. He stood above her as he said, "Blaezi, you've got to tell me."

The words came out before she could close her mouth. "I don't have to tell you anything if I don't want to."

He placed a hand on her shoulder and squeezed hard as he knelt beside her and breathed in her ear. "Yeah, you do." After she wriggled away from him, she still felt his warm, firm grip. She rubbed her ear to rid the tingling sensation his breath created.

"Well... since I don't have any Glamour anymore... and since you showed me the creek..." her voice cracked as she tried to control it. After a pause, her next words flowed without hesitation. Her face transformed into what she hoped was an accurate imitation of Queen Tania, and she made her voice sound as condescending as possible. "The terms of my exile are threefold. First, I'm to rid the Garden of Blight and Rottus. Second, I'm expected to solve the Naturals' problem." She broke character and said, "I'm assuming that's what you told everyone I'd do last night anyway." Her mimicry resumed. "Third, I'm to complete these tasks by the end of the second moon phase." Her face was void of emotion when she looked at him. "And I was only given three portions of Glamour with which to do all of this." She fought to appear emotionless. "And thanks to your river, I don't have any now."

Leaning back on his elbows, Thorne stared at the creek. "That's no small challenge." They didn't speak or move as the last of the sunrise's colors faded. Blaezi thought he'd fallen asleep. Then, he said, "Did they mean you're limited to those three portions, or is that just all they gave you?"

"Well, where else am I going to get it? It's not like you can steal Glamour." Why did she bother telling him anything?

He continued studying the water lapping its banks. "Actually, you can."

"Yeah, right." She snorted. "Even if I could, I'd just end up getting exiled from two bands of The People. I'd be the first one in lore to accomplish that!"

He was in her face again. "I said Glamour could be stolen, but I never suggested you should do it! A Faye, of all People, should know that."

"What's that supposed to mean?"

"You don't know a thing, do you?!" Thorne's temper flashed as bright as the morning before a cloud drifted across the sky, casting a shadow on his face. He sighed and said, "We can meet your terms."

Blaezi's wings perked and mouth dropped. "Are you serious?"

When Thorne gave her a quick nod, she leapt into the creek, kicking up water in triumph. Blaezi splashed Thorne and giggled, but when Thorne made a move toward the water, she paused mid-splash and yawned. "Can we talk about it later today, though? A Faye weighed down with moon dust can't fly." She shook her wings while the water reflected her silver hair turned green in the morning light.

Thorne said, "It wouldn't hurt to allow a little rest." He crashed through the water and splashed her. When they stopped to catch their breaths, he said, "You know, I could like this place if it weren't for that smell."

Blaezi sniffed the air. "What smell?"

"I'm not sure. I thought this might be something that *you* could tell *me* for once."

She breathed deeply. Her nose compared Natural smells to this one. Finally, she realized what he meant. She looked at him with what could have been sympathy or understanding.

"Do you know what it is?" asked Thorne. "Do you smell that?"

Blaezi nodded. "Humans."

CHAPTER 11

Arthur Axe was the sort of coach who wore shorts to school even in the winter. When it snowed, a black warm-up suit, sporting a silver knight, the school's mascot, was his favorite attire. Since he had graduated from Forrester High, he'd had a fierce loyalty to it. He liked being in a place where people remembered how many baskets he shot in a game fifteen years ago and commented on how proud they'd been when he received his full scholarship to Northern State. He cared a lot about the school, just not much about books.

A generous and easy going good ol' boy, he volunteered to do extra activities, such as summer school, as long as he got paid for it and didn't get chastised for not putting forth more effort. It wasn't that he didn't give students an education. For example, the pretty girls learned they could get A's if they flirted with sweet smiles during breaks. The druggies learned they could get D's if they left an occasional six pack or baggie in the floorboard of his always unlocked pickup truck—and kept their mouths shut during class. The athletes learned they had nothing to worry about in his or his buddies' classes since they charmed the counselors so their schedules worked out right. The students who looked as if they might be smart, even if they weren't, learned to fear him. His power left the nerds isolated. They were even afraid to sit too near each other.

School legend had it when Axe taught Driver's Education at summer school, he egged on pimply faced students in different cars, making up lies that one had said about the other concerning some online game. He provoked such a horrible fight one boy landed in the hospital from complications with an injury involving his eyeglasses. Other students, who were passengers in the cars, told their parents who told the principal. The worst punishment Mr. Axe received was that he no longer taught Driver's Education in the summer.

So that was how he became Kat's zoology teacher.

As usual, the bell sounded and Axe was nowhere to be seen. Kat sat at her desk, textbook opened, pen poised, and paper ready. When they heard footsteps, the cacophony of voices softened and all eyes looked toward the door. Duncan Hawk glided in, confident as usual, with a grin on his face. "You didn't think I was Coach, did you?" He announced to the room, "He's talking to construction people in the gym."

Forrester High was renovating their school gymnasium, and Axe spent most of his time there instead of in his classroom. Stopping at the seat in front of Kat, Duncan slung his bag on the floor. Kat watched every movement. His dark brown hair fell like feathers, reaching the top of his white t-shirt. He leaned forward and talked to the athletes in front of him and in the rows beside them.

After memorizing every strand of hair, Kat examined his ears and shoulders. His skin held the color of a perpetual tan and his white t-shirt managed to accent his skin as well as the muscles underneath it. He wasn't bulky, but had the muscles of someone who spent hours dribbling and shooting three-pointers, which he did. He was supposed to be the school's next big thing. Coach Axe had practically written him into his will. The Hawks had just moved to Forrester.

Duncan told his buddy, "Hey, man, did you see the board?" Scribbled in Axe's handwriting were instructions: Read Chapter 23 and do questions at the end. Duncan was very observant. He noticed assignments in class; he noticed openings on the basketball court—except, he never seemed to notice Kat. She groaned. The boys turned and looked at her.

Kat didn't know she'd made the noise out loud. Catching herself, she pursed her lips and pouted. "We haven't even reached 18 in our reading yet. How does King Arthur expect us to do Chapter 23?"

The guys laughed. "I don't know," one said. "I haven't done anything in here so far, and I'm not going to start now."

A boy wearing a summer soccer league t-shirt winked at her as she cringed. "You're cute," he said. "I don't see why you'd have to either." He looked at her forehead and said to his buddies, "If she can get rid of that horn."

Kat wanted to cry. She knew she had a few pimples, but making fun didn't help them go away any faster.

Duncan, however, examined her orderly desk. He looked her in the eyes and said, "Don't worry. Chapter 23 is mainly a review of parts of the other chapters. If you've kept up so far, you'll do okay." Before she could gush and act relieved, he swung around in his desk to rejoin his buddies.

Of *course* she had kept up so far. And like him, she knew what Chapter 23 consisted of because she had read it last week. What she couldn't figure out was how he knew. Coach Axe must give his players special outlines or assignments ahead of time. She'd heard the athletes all had files of the tests, too.

She didn't have any time to fume about that possibility because the man himself made an appearance. "Ladies and germs, are you ready to grade your papers?"

Scattered about the room, the studious individuals furiously wrote, trying to complete the assignment. Kat heard one worry to no one in particular, "We haven't had enough time!" Kat silently agreed and her stomach ached as she dreaded having to turn in an assignment unfinished. Only the boys in front of her seemed relaxed.

"Give us a break, Coach!"

"We'll turn it in tomorrow."

A pretty brunette on the front row looked up at him from beneath thick lashes. "Please?"

"Whatever. Quit your cryin'." Axe shuffled some papers on his desk. "I've got some business to attend to in the gym. But first, do you sugar britches have any questions about your ecosystems?"

Kat raised her hand. "Do we have to identify everything in it?"

"Is that the assignment?" he asked as he picked up papers, a baseball, a stapler, and a tennis shoe and inspected beneath them. He answered himself as he looked under a pack of cigarettes. "Why, yes, Coach, it is."

Kat persisted. "Do you have any suggestions for resources?"

Axe found what he'd been searching for—a clipboard with papers filled with x's and o's and squiggles. Basketball plays. "What kind of resources are you talking about?"

Kat was nervous. She hadn't meant for her questions to go on so long. The others stared. Changing her tactic, she smiled and tossed her blond hair. "What do you call those thingies that change colors to match their environment?"

The class decided to help.

"Snakes!"

"No, jerkwad. She's talking about lightning bugs."

"Those don't change colors." One boy flicked a pen at another one. "They just light up."

Duncan half-raised his hand as if he were taking a Boy Scout oath. "Coach, is she talking about chameleons?"

Axe, on his way out the door, walked over and clapped Duncan on the shoulder. "That's right, son. See, Kat, you don't need any of your resources after all." He was gone.

Duncan looked at her for the second time that morning. She worried he might see all of her secrets if she looked at his brown eyes too long. "Is that what you meant?" he asked, startling her into reality.

"Yeah," she said. "I think I've found a chameleon, but I can't seem to identify it. It's not like the ones in the books and online."

"Why?"

"For starters, it has wings."

CHAPTER 12

So far Blaezi had seen no humans, but she knew they were there. Thorne smelled them and so did she. Their homes weren't far away and more seemed to pop up like mushrooms each day. Since the Faye Council always arranged such things, she didn't know how to set up negotiations for the food and protection exchange for the Naturals. So she waited, hoping that when she met a human it would just happen. As the moon rose each night, she hoped redemption would come soon.

"There you are!" said Laurel as he loped up to Blaezi. "You've been at this creek every day since Thorne showed it to you."

"I know." Blaezi took a deep breath. "I don't like thinking about responsibility."

"Who does?" He shrugged his bony shoulders. "That's why I come here, too!"

"Yeah?" Wondering if he ever concerned himself with responsibility or was simply being kind, she smiled as he molded cobwebs into a sticky ball.

Pressing the web ball with his hands, he explained a new game idea. "This one's easy and a lot safer than Beeboarding." He nudged her when he used her word. "See, you stand under a tree and pick out a leaf." He pointed to a bright green one high above his head. "Then, players fly around to prevent opposing team members from hitting that leaf. You'll score if the web ball hits the leaf. It'll stick. Watch!" Laurel bent both legs and heaved the ball toward the tree leaves.

The icky mass of web didn't adhere to a single leaf but hurtled down to hit him in the face. He fell on the ground but kept chattering as if the ball were up on a leaf as he'd planned, instead of making parts of his body stick together. "Cool, huh?" He pulled the sticky web from his mouth.

"I'm surprised you don't like responsibility," he said, "being a Garden Guard and all." To avoid responding, she helped him remove the sticky webs from hair and wings. He continued, between spitting out bits of web. "And . .. ptttth... now you're... pwtttt. . . even going to help us work with the humans and save our for. . . pwtttthh... forest." He pulled the last strand from his tongue and said, "You seem pretty responsible to me."

"You never can tell." She shook her hand to loosen strands of web from her fingers. "I like coming here because this place reminds me of home. I miss it."

"Buzzlesnut. This place is so boring! I'm always having to make games to distract us so I don't fly right toward the sun and never stop!"

A frog hopped near the water's edge, and she heard its call. *Braaaagh!* Another jumped forward and its yellow throat was reflected in the creek.

Blaezi scrunched her nose. "Why doesn't that frog make any noise? I've noticed lots of them around here don't call."

Laurel worked to remove a particularly sticky mass clinging to his tail. "Either a disease or predator removes their tongues. We've been charming the frogs for summers upon summers so they can eat. Otherwise, no tongues, no food."

Blaezi flew over and patted the nose of the silent frog and then called out to Laurel. "Hey, weeping willow, you want a game? We play this at home all the time. It's called Leap Frog." She flew over to the noisy frog and hovered above him. "C'mon!"

Laurel, ready for anything, joined her and began leaping all around the vicinity of the frogs, using his wings to catch air and make his jumps higher.

Blaezi laughed at him. "No, you flea wannabe. Come up here like I am. There," she pointed at the noisy frog, "that one is yours."

Laurel hovered, his wings spread and mouth open in anticipation.

"When I say 'fly,' we're going to hop onto their backs and race. First, we need to claim a finish line."

"Oooh. That's a good one way over there." Laurel pointed to a tree on the other side of the creek.

"Making it hard, huh?" She raised her eyebrows at him. He just wiggled his wings. "You think you can cross the water? I'm not sure if you're up for this on your first try, but that's okay because I always win anyway."

"Oh, really?" asked Laurel, hands on hips. "Bring it on, Faye."

"Oh. It's on. Go!"

Blaezi and Laurel dropped full weight onto the unsuspecting frogs who leaped forward in surprise, then dove beneath the water. Blaezi reassured her frog, patting it, until it realized what was on its back. Soon, the frog surfaced and hopped onto the other side. Blaezi wooed the frog to stop and wait for Laurel. It was a race, but after all, it was his first time.

Seconds after she paused, Laurel and his frog burst from the water. His wings were wet but his smile was luminous. "Woohoo!" He held onto the frog with one hand and waved the other high in the air as they leapt ahead of Blaezi.

"Hey!" She pressed her frog with her heels.

Laurel and his frog tore across the rocks and up the incline of the creek bed. They were already into the tall grasses leading to the tree when Blaezi's frog, who had been gaining on them, froze. Without so much as a ribbit, Blaezi's frog turned completely around and frantically hopped the opposite direction. The last she saw was Laurel and his noisy frog leaping toward the tree. The only thing between Laurel and victory was a pair of human legs.

***

When Blaezi was about to be bounced back into the water by the frog, her wings took flight. She didn't know if she should go in search of Laurel or talk to the human. Since the moon was changing and she needed to meet her terms very soon, she opted to fly in the direction of the human. After all, the Naturals needed her help.

When she arrived near the tree, she watched the human, who seemed young and energetic. Like a Shasta daisy, flowers deceptive in their hardiness, she looked delicate with her white skin and yellow hair. In her hand, she held a sharp object with which she carefully sliced into the bark of the tree. It seemed she had been at work for a while because a number of chunks lay scattered on the ground.

"Stop! You're hurting it."

Kat's hand stilled and her head jerked to look over her shoulder. She didn't see anyone, so resumed her carving.

"You're hurting it," Blaezi called again. "Can't you see that?"

The human made a final cut, brushed away the excess, and stepped back to examine her handiwork. "It's bark falling to the ground. Not tears. Not blood."

"Exactly."

"Who's there?" Kat turned around and searched at eye level.

She saw nothing among the tangled branches of the forest, and then her eyes, narrowed and precise, lowered. At first sight of Blaezi, a change swept her face. Her curls bounced in the breeze, but her smile was about as close to the real thing as when a Faye's reflection looks back at her from the River. It was void of magic.

Kat crouched to better view Blaezi, who hovered above the poison oak a short distance from the tree.

"You talk?" Kat whispered.

"Yeah, ditzlesnit. And I said to stop hurting the tree. It's our forest, not yours."

Kat leaned up against the tree and crossed her arms, knife firmly curled in her fist. "I can't believe you talk. This is beautiful." Quickly then, she dropped her arms and leaned forward, "What do you eat?"

"What?" Blaezi sank an inch in flight. "That's what I wanted to talk to you about."

Kat shook her head and murmured, "I can't believe this." To Blaezi she said, "You wanted to talk to me?"

"Yes. We would like to offer negotiations for coexistence within our forest."

Kat patted her bulging pocket and, careful not to squash its contents, sat below the tree. This experience was completely bewildering. Who'd ever heard of a talking, flying chameleon?

"Sure. Um... who is offering these *negotiations?*" She couldn't believe the vocabulary on this thing.

Blaezi didn't know how the Naturals conducted business. The Fayes did everything by council, but that meant Tania took a few of them aside and told them what she wanted. The Naturals didn't even seem to have a leader and did pretty much whatever they wanted, speaking only for themselves. Blaezi figured she'd compromise. "I am Blaezi, a Faye, and I speak for myself."

Kat blinked. "Alright, Blaezi, a Faye, before I consider anything, you need to answer a few questions."

"Certainly," said Blaezi.

***

Much later, Kat shoved a chair up against the bedroom door handle. Breathless, she walked to her makeup counter and stared at the mirror. Triumph stared back at her. She reached for the box where she held her chameleons and released the hinge. She'd transferred them from the vivarium to a more secure area because with each addition to the collection the creatures grew friskier. It was almost as if they gained strength through numbers. Of course, from her interview she had also discovered they liked just about anything she herself ate. Food, obviously, strengthened them. And now she had another capture to add to her collection.

Wearing cargo pants that day had been a good idea. Unfortunately, only one of the pockets had been empty. Kat leaned over to unbuckle the wiggling cloth and scooped out her prize, throwing the new captive inside the box before slamming the lid on any possible escape.

CHAPTER 13

Sounds of revelry met Blaezi's ears before she reached the evening festival, enticing her to fly faster. Upon arrival, she pounced on Dogwood at the food line and said, "You're never going to believe this!"

Rock's voice emerged from behind them. "I've often felt if one says you're 'not going to believe' something—then you probably shouldn't."

"Save your grubby breath, Rock. I'm in too good a mood to let your sassafras bother me."

"Oh, no," said Rock. "And I thought that I was going to get to enjoy myself." He leaned close to Blaezi and sniffed her hair. "There's a beautiful moon out tonight, but..." he sniffed again, "you smell—"

"—like humans," said Thorne. He appeared from the other side of the mound of food Dogwood accumulated on the leaf he held in his hands.

Dogwood grinned sheepishly at her. "I wasn't going to say anything, Blaezi, but I think you've been spending too much time at the creek. Maybe you could roll around in the flowers some."

"Or poison ivy," said Rock.

Blaezi yelled, "Would everyone quit buzzing and let me say what I have to say?"

The food line stopped moving. All the nearby Naturals stopped and stared. Some held food almost at their lips, letting it hang in the air like fog.

She lowered her voice and the others resumed their former activities. "Dogwood. Thorne. I want to tell you what just happened. This is going to be great for all of the Naturals," she gazed at Thorne, "and for me."

"Did you meet a human?" Thorne asked.

"Yes! And we got to talking about negotiations and—"

Rock reappeared and exclaimed. "You spoke with a human?" He snorted. "Impossible!"

The news moved up and down the food line until everyone knew that Blaezi had supposedly spoken to a human. Those in the ring stopped dancing, and even the owls stared at her.

"I did!" cried Blaezi. "I spoke to her. We're meeting tomorrow night at the big tree by the creek to discuss further negotiations. I wasn't sure what you all wanted, so I told her we should meet under tomorrow's moon."

Thorne gave her a stern look and said, "Tell us exactly what happened."

"Okay." Blaezi put the story together in her head. "Laurel and I were playing Leap Frog, but my frog got scared and hopped away right when Laurel was about to win."

Rock sneered. "Typical of a Faye. When the going gets tough, you desert."

Blaezi tried to ignore him. "Anyway... my frog just dove into the creek and never came back. I flew back to look for Laurel, but I never found him again. Did he come back here?" She peered around the crowd of wings, searching for his goofy grin. "He'll tell you about that part."

"No," Rock said. "We haven't seen him tonight. As a matter of fact, several others are missing, too. They've been disappearing since just about the time you arrived."

Thorne turned to him. "Stop making accusations. You know Naturals often wander off to explore."

Rock crossed his arms. "All of them? Even—"

Thorne interrupted him. "She'll be back as soon as she's had all the berries she can eat." Thorne might have looked concerned, but Blaezi didn't notice.

Rock didn't forfeit. "I don't think so. Something is wrong. More and more Naturals are wandering off without telling anyone they've gone foraging." He jerked his chin toward Blaezi. "Since this has mostly happened since you brought *her* here, it's pretty strange, don't you think? Even you've got to admit that."

"I don't know what you two are talking about, but it's obvious everyone wants to hear what I have to say. Look at them." She motioned to the forest of faces surrounding them.

Rock became gracious and bowed with a flourish. "By all means, please tell us of your 'true' adventures and how you shall save us all."

Blaezi hovered, arms akimbo. "Okay, Mr. Waspy, I will. While I was looking for Laurel, I saw the girl standing at our finish line. We got to *talking*." She cast a stern look at Rock. "I realized how late it was and wanted to understand specifics on what you all desired, so I told her we'd have to meet tomorrow."

Rock bent over, laughing, gripping his stomach. "You're such a Faye. Not only do you lie, but you trust that she'll show up tomorrow. Fayes never finish a job."

"What do you mean?" Blaezi blinked back tears. Thorne just shook his head, turned his back, and flew away. She had been so happy, and now it seemed no one would even believe her.

Raine's voice came forth. "No, Rock. You are mistaken. Fayes can speak to humans. After all, if they work with them, they need to have the same language." He turned to Blaezi. "Go on. Tell us what happened."

She could have hugged the old Natural, wrinkled wings and all. There wasn't much left to tell, but she reveled in the attention. The only thing she didn't understand was why Thorne seemed angry with her.

CHAPTER 14

After dinner, Kat smuggled leftovers to feed the creatures. She set the paper plate on the vanity and opened the lid. The small beings slid near the food without even flitting their wings. Keeping a watchful eye on them, Kat opened her notebook, and wrote down her observations.

Journal Entry

Food: leftovers from dinner.

I found another one today near the big tree by the creek. This one TALKED. I didn't catch her, though. She made an appointment to meet with me tomorrow.

I caught another today—two sightings in one day! With each addition, they gain energy. They fly more often since the collection has grown. When I had only one captive, it stopped flying after a few days. The others rally around this new one and mimic his actions. He seems clumsier, but they still seem to follow him.

The phone rang in the hall. Her dad's bass voice seemed to carry on a long conversation with the person. Then, he called, "Kat, for you!"

"Who is it?"

"That Hawk boy."

Kat's face warmed and her stomach felt light and twisted—in a good way. Her mouth went suddenly dry.

Dad burst into the room holding a portable telephone. The

creatures shook their tails before becoming very still, and they gripped their food as if it might be taken away. Her father didn't see them, because they had again mimicked their surroundings. Tonight, they were primarily roast beef-mashed potatoes-green beans-colored. "Well?" asked her dad. "Do you want to talk to Ralph or not?"

Kat rushed to grab the phone out of his hand and gently used the door to push him from the room. She said, "His name's Duncan, Dad." She cringed at the thought of what her father might have said to him.

"Hi. This is Kat."

"Who is this Ralph guy?" Duncan's smile carried through the phone line.

"No one. My dad just likes to call people by wrong names. He thinks he's funny."

"I thought he was funny."

Kat offered a short laugh. "That makes two of you."

Silence hung on the line and she thought she heard a television in the background. She tried to figure out why Duncan, the cutest boy in her "zo" class and the most desired by the local newspaper and coaching staff, had called her. He must want her to do his homework. Or create his ecosystem.

Just when Kat had almost talked herself into getting angry at the silent boy on the other end of the telephone, he said, "I just watched this show on television."

"Yeah?" Good for you. It takes a real rocket scientist to sit in front of a TV, stuff his mouth with junk food, and scratch himself.

"*Yeah*," he mimicked. "It was about chameleons."

Kat sat up. Maybe he wasn't trying to get her homework. She sat back again and smirked. It had probably been a cartoon. She tried to recall any animated movies Disney had recently produced.

"Kat?" Duncan paused. "It wasn't *Attack of the Killer Chameleon* or anything."

"Oh. Sorry." She almost blushed at the thought that he might be able to read her mind. "What were you doing watching a show about lizards?" Had he been thinking of her as he flipped through the channels? And what about those nasty things made him think of her? Hey, at least he was thinking of her.

"It was on the Discovery Channel. They've got lots of cool shows. Prime time is always good. I love to watch it if practice doesn't run too late."

Kat sat silent. She never imagined this guy thought about anything besides bouncing balls. He had mentioned reading pretty far in the textbook, but she had assumed he'd taken the class before and flunked it.

"Am I calling at a bad time?" Duncan sounded disappointed.

"No!" Kat said a little too quickly. Then she walked over to her vanity and counted her captives, to ensure they had not escaped. "I'm just working on my project for class. You know, research." With the hand not holding the phone, she opened the lid of the box and began collecting and returning the creatures. They faintly fluttered their wings in her hands and wiggled their tails. If the phone call hadn't distracted her, she may have been surprised at the obedience with which they returned to the box.

"Research. That's what I'm calling about." So that's it. He wanted her to do his research. She whacked herself on the forehead—right where a zit the size of North America had formed. Ouch. "As I said, I just watched a show about chameleons. It was pretty detailed." He paused for effect. "No species had wings."

Kat was relieved he wasn't a homework moocher, but she was disappointed with his news. "Are you sure?"

"I'm not, but the Discovery Channel sure is." She heard his smile again. "I thought you'd want to know."

"Wow. Thanks. That'll save me from wasting more time on the wrong research. It was really nice of you to call... and to think of me."

"Yeah, well." The silence was in their rooms again. "I would have called your cell, but I didn't have your number. I found your home phone online."

Kat looked up and saw her reflection in the mirror. She couldn't believe what she saw.

Duncan continued. "Would you mind giving me your cell number just in case I... think of you... again."

"Sure!" Kat exclaimed. She couldn't believe this. She hurriedly gave him her phone number and threw in her instant message name for good measure. Although she was giddy that he had called, she longed to conduct more experiments with her specimens.

"Well, I guess I'll see you in class tomorrow," said Kat.

"I'll try to be on time. Maybe we could discuss your project a little more."

"Okay." What? Did he think that was the only thing she was capable of discussing? Sure, she was surprised *he* could discuss it, but she knew a little about sports and other stuff, too.

"And, ya know. . . if you want. . . I could come over and check out your 'winged chameleon' sometime." Duncan hesitated. "I watch a lot of nature shows."

"I might like that." She hoped she sounded flirtatious and not insulting. Duncan laughed, so she figured she was safe. She hurried to hang up on a good note. "I'll catch you tomorrow, Ralph. Er. I mean, *Duncan*."

They both laughed as the connection broke. Her skin felt tingly and warm. She didn't know if it was from talking to him or what she saw in the mirror. Where she had smacked her forehead, there was no North America. No horn. No pimple. No pain. She looked closely. The clear skin was where her fingers had touched. And the only things she had touched before her head... were the creatures.

***

Journal Entry

It seems these things have a healing power or something that makes acne disappear. Moreover, they seem to make inanimate objects appear prettier. Tonight, I took several of them one at a time and shook them like dice between my hands. For experiment number 1, I applied my hands to my hair, and my hair instantly looked fabulous, like a magazine ad. On experiment 2, I brushed my fingers across an old t-shirt, and it seems new. (I'll wear it tomorrow morning.)

Residue remains on my hands after I handle the specimens until it falls off onto something else. The residue is invisible to the untrained eye, but on closer examination I can see the sparkles. The interior of their box is thick with it. I brushed a bit on my makeup brush and across my face. All of my pimples disappeared! More than that, though, I just look... better.

An unfortunate turn of events occurred, however. The creatures have been so calm and docile since I caught the last one. I was conducting more experiments this evening with them when, all of a sudden, they went berserk. I had become a little lax with security and left my bedroom door ajar. They flew everywhere and several escaped before I could slam the door. That's when I heard a snap. The door had cleanly knocked off one of their tails. No blood was visible. I will need to hunt more tomorrow afternoon.

Kat closed her journal and placed it behind her bed, between the books of fairy tales she'd had since childhood. She picked up the tail and held it against her lips. It was so beautiful and felt nice.

She wondered how Duncan's lips might feel, then embarrassed, moved to her vanity. Since the tail was soft and pretty, she put it in the jar with her make up brushes—after she brushed it all over her face. She looked in the mirror and smiled a smile that wasn't just for practice.

CHAPTER 15

Blaezi hadn't seen Thorne all day. Nor had she seen him last night after Rock had made him annoyed with her. At least, she figured it had to be Rock. She hadn't done anything wrong, had she? Well, she couldn't think of any of that right now. She had spoken to Raine and the others. There was one thing for her to focus on now—the human.

Each time Blaezi heard a bird call or a twig snap, she was sure the human was returning to discuss negotiations. Long past the time she had seen her the day before, Blaezi waited, patient for once. She needed to help the Naturals before she could return home. Sure, she had to rid the Garden of Blight and Rottus somehow, but she would think about that later. One acorn at a time, as the squirrels say. She feared another moonlit night would pass without speaking to the human. Another night lost would be one evening closer to permanent exile. If she didn't help the Naturals, they might discover her true situation and cast her out, alone. Blaezi shivered at the prospect, knowing she wouldn't last long. Most Solitaries didn't. A positive negotiation was her only chance for either of the outcomes she desired. Blaezi's thoughts were interrupted while she planned her next contact strategy.

"Help us!" a whisper flew on the breeze.

Blaezi's wings perked up as she identified the direction of the call.

"He---lp... ussssssss!" The voice called again. "Pleeeeease...

help!"

Laurel and a small cluster of Naturals struggled to stay air bound as they stumbled over themselves. Some carried weaker ones and their wings seemed to do little to ease the weight. Blaezi had never before seen one of the People so dangerously ill.

She ran to Laurel and gripped his hand. Many of the Naturals with him were unknown to her. These must be the ones Rock mentioned who had been missing since her arrival. Of course, Laurel was playing with her just yesterday, and he looked pretty bad. Was she responsible in some way?

A sob caught her voice. She forced the words. "What happened?" He offered a shadow of his grin, and Blaezi found comfort in the fact he was still able to smile.

"A human." His usually jovial manner was grim. She'd never seen him like this. Something had altered him.

Before she could ask any more questions, Thorne appeared from the weeds. Blaezi wondered if he had been spying on her, but didn't mind when she looked at the empty eyes of the Naturals sinking so close to the ground. A light seemed to return when Thorne neared them. After flinging a portion's worth of Glamour above their heads, he heaved one Natural across his shoulders and lifted one of the sickest into his arms. Her long, silver tail hung limp, but Blaezi thought it looked vaguely familiar. Before all of the pixie dust had had a chance to settle, Thorne called over his shoulder as he zipped toward camp, "I'll be back with more help."

"I'm sorry I don't have any Glamour to help ease the pain or make it better," muttered Blaezi as she studied the ground. She didn't like the absent look in most of their eyes. She felt stupid for losing her portions in the river.

Laurel squeezed her hand and said, "If your Glamour doesn't soon return stronger than ever, then I don't know tails."

What an odd thing to say. The poor guy must be delirious. He undoubtedly knew stories; he seemed to be the leader of games and entertainment after all. What did *tales* have to do with Glamour?

His explanation was preempted when Thorne returned with Dogwood and others. They hurried to gather the bedraggled group and rush them back to camp. Laurel put out a hand and brushed the air with a motion that told Dogwood to scat when he offered assistance. "I need to speak to Thorne." Laurel attempted a deep, difficult breath. "And Blaezi." He puffed out his chest in mock bravery and forced a semblance of his goofy grin. "I'm fine. Take the others to camp and heal them. They are almost completely absent of Glamour. Some have been held prisoner for nearly a full moon cycle."

When Dogwood and the others departed, Thorne threw Laurel's arm over his shoulder and motioned to Blaezi to do the same with his other. Laurel didn't object. They flew back to the tree where Blaezi was supposed to meet the human. And where Blaezi had last seen Laurel. When they arrived, they paused and Thorne produced a flask of water. Laurel gulped before collapsing, eyes closed, with his back against the tree.

"That was goo-ood." Laurel opened his eyes and his body stiffened as he recognized where he was.

"We need to leave here." He glanced in the direction of the human dwellings and sniffed the air. "She'll be back soon."

Thorne and Blaezi exchanged looks.

"Do you mean the human Blaezi has set up negotiations with?" Thorne asked.

Blaezi smiled inside. So he had believed she spoke to humans. What had caused his anger with her?

"Yes. I couldn't understand it, but I heard them talking. I was in the human's pocket."

Blaezi sucked air into her lungs. She thought she had seen the girl's clothing twitch. While Laurel struggled to free himself, Blaezi had noticed and done nothing to help.

"I'm sure she plans to return. Especially since so many of us escaped."

"You mean others were left behind?"

He hung his head. "We couldn't all leave. I tried, but it didn't work."

Thorne asked, "What happened? Please tell us." He put his hand on his friend's shoulder. His face was expressionless except for the hint of tears forming in his eyes.

Laurel said to Blaezi, "That was a fun game you showed me, until the end. My frog leapt out of control. At first I thought you'd bewitched it so you could win." He attempted a smile but it quickly dimmed. "But now I think it sensed the human and knew it was evil. The next time I see one, I'll run, too." He took another drink of water. "She did things to us." His eyes filled with the vacant look most of the others' had held. "I don't know what was done to those who'd been there longest." His voice faded, but then he caught himself and strengthened it so that they could hear. "We were kept in a dark cave with a tight closure. No light or nature was near us. To be expected, each Natural seemed to gain strength when more of us arrived. However, with no moonlight and no contact with the land..."

"How did you get away?" asked Blaezi.

"A game." He shrugged. "I told the others to be very still and move like turtles until our opportunity arrived. That way the human wouldn't expect us to fly away. They had been trying to escape at every opportunity and it had weakened them. We caught her off guard."

Thorne asked, "What did she want?"

"I don't know if she even knew." Laurel raised his sad eyes and shrugged. "But she will now. And she'll want more. She..." He lifted his rump from the ground and patted his bottom. "She got my tail."

CHAPTER 16

After school, Kat was in a hurry to go to the creek to meet the talking... thingy. Just as she walked inside her house, her phone buzzed in her backpack. When she recovered it from beneath a large notebook, she saw a text message.

F2T

Duncan? Absolutely positively without a doubt she was *free to talk*. She'd only stared at his back through the entire class today and he'd barely spoken to her except to say "you're welcome" when she thanked him for his call. He'd acted almost shy. She pushed the numbers on her phone: 9-3-7. *Yes*.

☺

Well, she was pretty darn happy, too. That warm feeling began in her stomach again. Then he sent another message.

WYGOWM?

Her hands began to sweat and she blinked at her phone several times. Duncan just moved here. Maybe that meant something else where he was from. He must have realized she didn't understand because he sent another message:

Can you IM?

Kat raced to her computer and opened her instant messenger. As soon as she logged in, she saw that he was already online.

Hawk: hi
Kiddykat: Hi back.

There was a pause.

Hawk: so...? you didn't answer my question

Kat took a deep breath and typed. Her fingers slipped off the keys, forcing her to correct typos before sending.

Kiddykat: I'm not sure what you meant.
Hawk: will you go out with me?
Hawk: Tonight?
Hawk: we could work on our ecosystems if you want

Kat couldn't tell if he was nervous and wanted to go out with her, or if he was still trying to use her for her brain. Then again, she did manage to keep it pretty well hidden in class.

Kiddykat: Well...I had plans with Ralph, but...
Hawk: sorry
Hawk: never mind. I thought your dad just made him up. I didn't know he was real

Kat laughed. She liked messing with his head. Guys were such interesting studies.

Kiddykat: He's not real. I was joking. What time?

There was a long wait before the next message popped up. Kat thought she might have made him angry. Then the message indicator sounded, and she surmised that she hadn't.

Hawk: could I pick you up at 7:00? we have

practice until 6

Kat figured she'd just about let him do anything he wanted but wrote instead:

Kiddykat: Sounds pretty good.
Hawk: I'd like to see where you found your winged chameleons. ;)

Kat laughed.

Kiddykat: :p Sure. Maybe we could find some more.
Hawk: don't eat dinner. I've got plans

Kat smiled. She could appreciate a man with a plan.

Kiddykat: Do you need directions to my house?
Hawk: Nope

Kat stared at her computer screen and tried to figure out who he had asked for directions.

Hawk: internet. I got your phone number, remember? also picked up a map. I now know all of the names of your neighbors, too. ☺
Kiddykat: That's a little creepy.
Hawk: ☺
Hawk: GTG

Kat blinked in disappointment at his abrupt mood swing, and the corners of her mouth threatened a frown.

Hawk: practice starts in 15

Oh. Of course, he had to shoot hoops and have Coach Axe blow whistles at him. She smiled. She couldn't blame Axe. After all, she wouldn't mind whistling at Duncan, either.

Kiddykat: See you at seven.
Hawk: BTW you looked really nice today

He went offline. She felt all warm again and knew she was blushing. She turned around in her desk chair and looked at her vanity. With relief she could still see the creature's tail tucked in with her makeup brushes. Good. She could look "really nice" again tonight.

She squealed, clapped her hands together and rushed into the kitchen for an after school snack. The creek and talking creature temporarily forgotten.

***

At 7:00 sharp, Kat's doorbell rang. Although she was ready and used the tail to make sure she "looked nice," she let her parents answer the door. As soon as she heard Duncan's voice, however, fear gripped her stomach. Perhaps she shouldn't leave him with her parents too long. Who knows what they might say?

She ran down the hallway and slowed herself before coming into view of the living room. From the doorway, she glanced at the three of them. Her parents sat in their respective armchairs and sipped tea. Duncan sat across from them on the couch. His elbows were fixed on his knees as he leaned forward and spoke. When Kat appeared, they stopped talking. Her parents appeared a little in awe of her, but she didn't notice. Duncan abruptly stood. Then he sat. Then he stood again and said, "Kello, Hat." He looked at the carpet and then corrected himself with, "Hello, Kat."

"Hi." Kat smiled, savoring the effect she seemed to have on this boy. He must like her after all.

As usual, Duncan surveyed everything and his eyes swept her. He stopped at her shoes. "You look great."

Her mom interrupted their moment. "Honey, based on what Duncan's told us you'll be doing tonight, you should change."

Her dad took a sip of tea and nodded. "For safety's sake, thongs are an inappropriate choice."

"Dad!" Kat cried. "Mom? A little help here?"

"Your father and I agree," she said. "A thong falling off might get you into more than one kind of trouble."

Duncan's eyes widened to almost the size of Kat's. She had that warm sensation in her stomach again. Duncan remained calm as he grinned. "Yeah, tennis shoes or boots might be better than those." He pointed to her flip flops. Oh yeah, *thongs.*

Kat gave her parents a disdainful look. "Sure, I'll be right back."

When she returned wearing pink canvas sneakers, her parents seemed at ease again, and Duncan's feathers didn't seem to be ruffled, either.

"Do I look all right now?" She posed in the doorway,

Duncan smiled. "Perfect."

He opened the front door for her, and she couldn't believe what she saw in the driveway.

CHAPTER 17

Kat wasn't sure if she liked the smell of the horse, but she *was* sure she liked the smell of the guy riding behind her with his hands loosely holding the reins. Even though she'd grown up in Oklahoma, where many assumed the state's inhabitants rode horses to school, she'd never even touched one. Although she'd been a little nervous when he boosted her onto the saddle, she felt safer knowing he was behind her. When she moved just right, her back touched the front of his chest. They rode in the direction of the creek.

"This is nice and all, Duncan, but... don't you have a car?"

"Sure," he said. "The war pony's getting new shoes."

Puzzled, she tried to turn in the saddle to look at him, but he nudged her shoulder and laughed. "Face forward." She did as she was told. He explained, "My *car's* getting new *tires*. I thought this would be fun. Besides, we're working on our ecosystems, right?"

Kat nodded.

"Well, this is a good way to explore more area. I can't exactly take my Mustang down to the creek."

She giggled as she imagined a shiny sports car with new tires bounding through the fields behind her house.

"Plus," he said. "It's not like people will be able to do this much longer. I hear this whole area is becoming a housing addition."

"Yep," Kat replied. "Right up to the creek." Kat's stomach

growled and they both laughed.

Duncan said, "I'm hungry, too. Coach worked us hard today. We'll eat when we reach the creek." He clucked to the horse, their speed increased and the ride became bumpier.

She wondered if they were going to forage for roots and berries. It wasn't like there was a McDonald's nearby. However, she said, "How do you like playing ball here? How do you like Forrester?"

"I like playing with the team. I mean, it's cool to be a part of something that is so established and successful."

"We've made it to the state championships the last..." Kat tried to count the years with each bump, but became frustrated, "...forever years in a row."

Duncan laughed. "Sure, but who else practices in the off-season like we do?" He became serious when he said, "Of course, because of state restrictions it's not like we're really practicing for the school. It just so happens that we're on a league team with all of the same players and the same coach."

"Axe knows how to manipulate the system alright," said Kat. She rather admired him for it.

The creek came into view and Duncan reined in the horse and hopped off. "Swing your right leg over," he instructed. She did, and he reached up, wrapping his hands around her waist, and lifted her off the horse and onto the ground. He still had his hands around her waist when he said, "Oh. And to answer your other question," his eyes skimmed her face, "I like Forrester just fine."

CHAPTER 18

"You must tell the others," insisted Thorne. "A human in possession of one of our tails is dangerous." He and Laurel looked at Blaezi, and she nodded as if she understood. She frowned and pursed her lips.

Laurel answered, "I know." He studied Thorne and said, "I did my best to take care of... all the People, especially—"

"I'm sure you did. She... *they*... will be fine as soon as Raine sees them."

Blaezi tired of being ignored. "Listen, if you need to talk in private, just say so. I hate it when Naturals try to talk around me like I'm too much of a slug to get that they're doing it!"

Thorne's wings turned red. At first Blaezi thought he was embarrassed, then she realized he was angry. Laurel laughed a little like his old self and said, "I'll let you two deal with this issue. I'm going to see Raine." Laurel stood and eased toward camp.

Blaezi tossed her hair and stared at Thorne. "What? You are sooooo moody."

Thorne's voice was steady. She noticed he often sounded very calm at his angriest. "You are oblivious to what is going on around you." He turned to follow Laurel.

Blaezi flew until she hovered before him. "Stop! You were mad at me last night when Rock harassed me about meeting with the human and sharing what I thought was good news." Thorne flew over her. Blaezi went after him again and placed herself in his path. "Stop! I mean it. NOW."

Thorne began to fly around her again until she yelled, "What is wrong with you?"

His emotions poured forth like a spring. "Just when I thought I could trust you... you act like yourself!"

Blaezi's wings riffled. "And what's wrong with me?"

Thorne looked her up and down and said, "What's *right?*" He did fly around her this time, looked back at where her tail should be and snorted.

Blaezi flew to the ground, picked up a clump of dirt, and threw it at his ankles. His momentum was thrown off, sending him feet over head until he hit the soft grass. Blaezi flew to him.

"Did you forget I'm a Garden Guard?!" Blaezi spat as she stood over him. "Nothing gets by me."

Thorne jumped to his feet. "Until you decide to go to Midsummer Festival or some other party!"

Blaezi stared at him with narrowed eyes. "That was before. I'm different now. You of all the People should know that."

"Well, I don't." Thorne clinched his fists. "The Fayes probably had good reason to banish you."

"You're crazy!" Blaezi picked up another clod of earth and threw, but he dodged it by flying an inch higher. "And you're the meanest Natural I've ever known!"

Thorne forced a laugh as he swept toward her and restrained her arms with his own so she couldn't throw anything else. "If I'm crazy, then why aren't I the one who is banished? I should have known you'd do the same thing here."

She struggled to free herself, but Thorne was strong. "Same thing?"

He moved so close that his nose touched hers. She felt his

breath when he said, "You didn't know then that the human was evil. You left the human when you thought it could have *saved* us. You chose to go to our evening festival instead and acted like you did it for us." His lip curled in disgust. "Rock was right."

She stopped struggling and blinked at him, fully aware of what he had understood to be true as well as how close they were to each other. Thorne must have noticed their proximity, too, because he dropped her arms and backed away.

Rubbing where he had gripped her, she said, "I didn't leave for a party."

Thorne said, "Oh."

Blaezi continued. "You're partly right, though."

"I thought so!"

"I did lie." She glared at him and raised her chin. "I wanted to take care of everything that night, but the girl wanted to wait until today. But I didn't want everyone thinking I was incompetent, and so you wouldn't get into trouble for bringing me from the Fayes, I said *I* had made the decision." Her eyes teared and she hung her head. "She'd already caught Laurel and was probably planning to come back and get me."

"You're right." The wind blew and he sniffed the air. "She was planning to come for you. And she's here." Thorne grabbed her hand, and, together, they flew toward camp, collecting Laurel on their way.

As soon as they were out of sight, Rock peered over the roots of the tree protruding from the earth. "Banished?" He laughed and slapped his thigh. "This is too good! Wait until I tell the others. Raine won't think you're such a great Natural when he learns you've brought us discarded goods!" Rock was still laughing, eyes closed, when the shadow loomed over him.

Chapter 19

Kat zipped her purse and abruptly smacked it against the tree trunk as Duncan, holding a blanket and a couple of saddle bags, returned from tying the horse.

He laughed. "Did your purse attack you or something? You look like you're doing a good job of showing it who's boss."

Kat blushed. "No! I caught another...." She looked at Duncan's eyes and quickly looked away. Something told her she shouldn't show him her creatures. Sure, he might be able to help her identify them, but, somehow, she didn't think he'd approve. "I caught another..." she swallowed hard, "mosquito. I just smacked it with my purse." She gave her bag a swipe with her hand and said, "There. Now it's all gone." She looked at what he was holding. "What are those for?"

He set his things on the ground and spread the blanket. "I told you I had dinner plans."

Reaching inside the saddle bags, Duncan removed peanut butter and jelly sandwiches, chips, grapes, and two bottled waters.

"Wow." Kat twirled her blond hair around her finger. "I thought you were just a stud basketball player. I didn't know you were a chef, too."

Duncan raised an eyebrow as he gave her a paper towel. "You thought I was a stud?"

She changed the subject. "Oh, I have some hand sanitizer before we eat."

His eyes widened as he leaned away from her. "And I thought I'd planned for everything."

She removed a couple of packets from a side pocket of her purse and threw one at him. "Hey, don't worry. Nobody's perfect!"

"Is that what you think?"

"Yes, Mr. Charming, I do." He offered her a bottle, and she smiled. "But some of us are closer than others." He grinned at her and she studied the lines of his neck and how they met his defined collarbone.

He said, "You seem pretty close."

She almost dropped the slippery water bottle.

He winked at her. "I mean it. You're kind. For example, you didn't have to help that guy in class with his assignment."

Kat hadn't done it out of kindness. The boy's labored nasal breathing each time he got stuck on a question had annoyed her since they were in third grade.

Duncan continued. "You're smart—I don't know how you answered that question in class today about that guy from the middle ages."

Kat blushed. "Edward Edward Wotton? Now, he was a smart guy. He ignored all the fanciful folklore and went back to the basics of studying nature. He wasn't interested in fairy tales. He wanted science."

"The perfect zoologist?"

"Maybe." She looked him in the eyes. "Here's my philosophy," she said, "I think no one's *born* perfect, but they can certainly be made to *look* that way."

Duncan lifted his water bottle. "To perfection," he said.

Her eyes glittered as she clunked her bottle to his. "To

beautiful perfection."

***

When Blaezi and Thorne returned to camp for the evening festival, the former prisoners appeared healthier. Surrounded by friends and Glamour, their ability to fly short distances increased, and they inhaled food as if starved for the duration of their captivity. Because their bodies had not yet recovered, each gleamed an unusual shade of pink. Thorne left Blaezi with Raine to talk to them.

"This is scary. I've never known of humans hunting the People before," said Blaezi.

Raine slowly turned his head to look at her, and then he stared back out at the returned Naturals talking to Thorne. "The Fayes have not shared the stories from the old land."

"What do you mean?" asked Blaezi. "What 'stories'? What 'old land'?" She shook her head. "I thought we were always from the River."

"No, young one," said Raine. "You are mistaken."

"Why do you know and I don't? I'm a Faye." Blaezi realized she sounded disrespectful but she didn't care. "Why do you know my lore and I don't?" He wasn't one to lie. What did Raine know about predators of Fayes?

"I know well those who were there." He continued to study the group of happy Naturals clamoring over each other to grab more food before the dancing began.

"Don't just stand there!" cried Blaezi. "Please tell me."

Raine's face possessed a calm Blaezi had never known. "I will tell you and the others." He continued his observation of the party. "But not now. No, they are not ready to be reminded yet." His glance returned to her once more. "And you," he said, "need to learn patience."

CHAPTER 20

When they finished their dinner, Duncan scooped all of the trash into the saddle bags, but left the remaining grapes and food. "Just in case any animals don't feel like fixing dinner tonight."

Duncan and Kat walked to the horse and untied him. "You want to take a walk along the creek and check out stuff for our ecosystems?"

"Sure," she said and clutched her purse.

Duncan's horse followed like a puppy.

"Won't he run away if you're not holding on to him?" asked Kat.

He reached back and patted the horse's neck. "Nope. He respects me too much for that."

Kat giggled. "You have the respect of a horse?"

"Sure," Duncan said. "You have to respect and earn the respect of nature before you can get the most benefit from it."

Whatever. Kat shot him a look. Oops. He was serious. Oh well. Nobody's perfect.

When they reached the creek, the horse dipped his head to drink.

Since Duncan seemed to be "into" the nature thing, Kat said, "This creek runs right into the Illinois River." He looked toward the sun. "Do we have time to scope it out?"

"Sure." Kat checked her watch. "The sun won't set for another hour."

The river was rocky, so Duncan tied his horse to a tree as they walked along the riverbed. Kat was glad she hadn't worn her flip flops or she'd have been fighting pebbles.

Duncan reached into the water, removed a stone, and held it up to the sky. "Look, the river made this hole through it. Can you imagine how many years it took to do that?"

"Cool!" breathed Kat as she peered into the sky through this stone telescope. This guy may like nature, but he also seemed to appreciate scientific progress. "Let's find more. I think I want to put them in my ecosystem."

"Me, too," he said.

They kept their eyes peeled on the rocks beneath their feet. The water grew swift around a bend, and as time passed, Kat became more intense in her search. She figured where the water ran swifter, the likelihood of finding more rocks with holes increased.

Just a short distance from shore, a rock about the size of her foot protruded from the white water. Staring at it, she contemplated whether or not she could maintain her balance and reach into the river. Again happy she had worn sneakers and not sandals, she leapt onto the rock and realized, too late, she hadn't calculated that the rock would be slippery. Her arms flapped as she tried catching her balance. She let out a shriek, "Sheeeiiiioooo!" She closed her eyes and mouth tightly, held her breath, and waited for water. Instead of hitting the water, though, she hit Duncan's chest.

His jeans were wet to the knees, but she was dry and being carried onto shore. "You should be more careful," he grinned. "I won't always be here to save you from yourself."

She let out her breath. "Oh yeah?" She wrapped her arms around his neck. "Who says I need to be saved?"

He set her on a large rock jutting from the riverbank, and she reluctantly loosened her hold of him. He leaned over and wrung the water from the legs of his jeans.

Twirling her hair, she flashed a smile. "Sorry you had to 'save' me." But she enjoyed it, so she wasn't that sorry.

He looked at her and said, "Don't worry. You're worth it."

"You bet I am."

When he had done as much as he could, he sat up straight and said, "You know what my aunt would have said about what just happened?"

Kat shook her head. She was more interested in the muscles in his caramel colored arms than in his family.

"She would have said the Little People were pulling a trick on you. They often pull girls into water who get too close." He laughed and stood. Kat watched him move. "We should head back. It will be dark soon, and I don't exactly have headlights."

On the horse and moving toward home, Kat was able to collect her thoughts. Concentration was easier when Duncan was out of sight. Unfortunately, she could still hear him whistling.

Kat interrupted his song. "What was your aunt talking about?" she asked. "Little people like on *The Wizard of Oz*?"

Duncan didn't answer for a few more paces of the horse. "No," he said, "it's an American Indian thing. She's Cherokee." And then he was silent.

"Oh," she said and echoed his silence.

***

Naturals lolled on the grasses before the dancing began. Raine flew to the center of the group. He waited. After a moment, the others stopped chattering and focused on him.

"Thank you for your attention. The evening is new and much amusement yet to be had." The Naturals cheered. Raine paused until quiet returned. "Sadly, we must first discuss unhappy experiences so we may not repeat them."

Blaezi looked over at the still pink-tinged Naturals, surrounded by friends. They sat very still and listened to Raine. Blaezi shivered with the realization she could have been captured... and that some of the People remained in the human girl's possession.

Raine continued. "On rare occasion, the Naturals have been known to interact with nature loving humans, usually children who need our help. These gentle humans are too few in numbers these moons for us to seek them in our current situation, so Thorne summoned Blaezi. As a Faye, she knows more how to deal with humans like those nearby."

A few Naturals looked to Blaezi with grateful smiles. Some mouthed the words "thank you." Blaezi observed a few had fashioned their hair and wings after hers. Dogwood patted her on the back, and Laurel clapped for her from across the forest floor. Thorne, sitting beside Laurel and the other injured Naturals, nodded to her.

Raine took a deep breath. "A great need for caution exists. We may be in danger, but there is no need for fear. The first human who made contact with us is an enemy to the Natural world." He let his words sink in before saying, "Some of you may not have heard, but the human possesses Laurel's tail."

Gasps bounced from leaf to leaf. An older Natural sobbed. Blaezi and the very young ones looked apathetic. Why should there be a big storm about a tail?

CHAPTER 21

Kat and Duncan stood at the foot of the steps that led to her front porch. She wasn't sure what to do next, so she sat on a step and said, "Do you want to have a seat?"

He glanced at the setting sun. "Sure, for a minute." He sat beside her. "We haven't had dessert, you know."

Her body tensed. Weren't the grapes dessert?

"I have a kiss for you."

Her breath caught in her chest. He was forward. A real go-getter. Before she could embarrass herself by puckering up and closing her eyes, which was what she was an eyelash away from doing, he reached into his pocket and pulled out a couple of gently melted Hershey's kisses.

He smiled as he placed one on her bent knee.

"Thanks." She popped it in her mouth and chewed, hoping he wouldn't sense her embarrassment but knowing he did. "Mmmm." She swallowed and ran her tongue across her teeth to cleanse them of chocolate. "Nothing like a chocolate kiss to end a perfect dinner."

"Perfect, huh?" he whispered and leaned close to her.

"Beautifully," she replied.

Next, she felt the soft touch of the horse's nose as he leaned down and nuzzled both of their cheeks. Duncan laughed and stood. "I think it's time to go. I'll see you tomorrow morning in class."

When Kat moved to go inside, Duncan reached out to cup her jaw with his palm while his fingers curled around the back of her neck. With his other arm, he pulled her to him. Softly, carefully, he kissed her. Before releasing her he whispered, "Now it's a perfect evening, beautiful."

As the crickets sang, Kat waved Duncan down the driveway, then she flew into her room and unloaded her purse.

CHAPTER 22

The Naturals listened in awe to Raine as he created detailed images of past horrors. Blaezi had trouble connecting with the tale, even though he was telling of the Fayes. She didn't know her own lore.

"Many, many midsummers ago, when I was as young as you," he pointed at Blaezi, "and you," he turned to point at Thorne, "I met the Fayes for the first time. They were not the pompous, un-Natural creatures we hear of now. Instead, they resembled much more our own who returned to us just this evening." He gestured toward the huddle of pinkish Naturals.

"Long ago, before humans flew on wheels of thunder that traveled on rivers of stone, Fayes came. Before the humans with skin the color of snow and evening and sun appeared, we only knew of the humans of earth. The animals knew them as we knew the animals, and we respected each other. After the Fayes came, the humans of earth dwindled, and the humans of snow and evening and sun grew in population.

"The Fayes came to us for help. They hungered and lacked Glamour. They carried their Glamour in sacks to protect it. What made their travel more difficult, of course, was that not one of them had a tail."

None of the Fayes had tails. Queen Tania ordered they be removed during each moon. If it made life more difficult, why would she do that?

"As we all know, a primary source of Glamour is in our tails." Naturals all around Blaezi nodded, but Blaezi was confused.

"The Fayes long interacted with humans in their old land. Much of their relationship was built on mystery and fear. They played many jokes on the humans as well as helped them, and the Fayes were cared for. Food was left out for them by humans, and a general respect was assumed—until one fateful day." Raine paused, and a young Natural offered him a dew drop to cure his dry throat. Raine patted the young one's shoulder and continued.

"Besides removing their tails, they were forced to make other changes. Before they adopted our term of the People, they called our species *fairies*. A pair of human brothers captured some Fayes. These brothers were tellers of human lore and scholars of human language. As expected, some stories were purely entertaining while others were true." He smiled. "At the time that they caught the Fayes, they used human magic to retell their stories."

Blaezi hadn't known humans possessed magic. As if reading her mind, Raine spoke to her. "See, they used a special stick," he reached down and grabbed a twig, "and with it made marks to enable whoever looked at the markings next to know the same story."

Some of the young Naturals, who had crept closer to crouch at Raine's feet, *oohed*, and the older ones nodded as if they'd seen this magic themselves. Blaezi had seen this. It wasn't magic. What did the humans call it... writing? Also, she'd seen the human girl making such markings on the tree before she spoke to her.

"Much like Laurel and our brave Naturals, the first Faye escaped. When he flew away, though, one of the brothers slammed down hard on him with a great collection of these magic markings that weighed as much as a rock."

"A book!" Blaezi said the foreign word herself, proud she had remembered the name.

"Thank you, Blaezi." Raine smiled at her. "He slammed down hard on him with 'a book,' but the part he hit was the tail. The rest of the Faye got away."

"What happened next is unknown to us, but the humans somehow learned of the power of the tail. Perhaps they placed it inside... a *book* and it transformed the story, or perhaps they began making marks with the tail at that moment. We know they did so later." Raine shrugged. "No matter. We do know that they eventually hunted Fayes for their tails."

Blaezi could hardly believe what she was hearing. The humans she had known in the Garden had been so kind. It even seemed fair that since Blight and Rottus had taken over, they refused to feed the Fayes anymore. She struggled to believe all humans could be cruel.

"The brothers received great acclaim for their lore. However, as we all know, stealing Glamour can have its consequences. All must pay who use Glamour that does not belong to them."

The Naturals all nodded. Some grunted approval.

"All of the lore the brothers shared exposed the grim realities of human nature. The stories are known to humans even after so many generations. Humans devour them with all of their cruel truths about mankind."

Blaezi whispered to Dogwood, "Were the Fayes... banished from their home because they lured fairy hunters to the woods?"

Raine seemed to know all that occurred within reach of his senses. He looked at Blaezi and shook his head without the rest of the Naturals ever hearing her question. "The brothers held many hunts, collecting stories and tails along the way. Many troupes were hunted over a vast area, and a few bands of People were lost forever."

Blaezi gasped.

"So the Fayes decided to escape. They flew as far as they could from human hands. When they came to our forest, we welcomed them and helped them learn how to feed themselves naturally. They had never had to rely solely on themselves before."

What could have happened to make the Fayes resent the Naturals so much? If the Naturals helped the Fayes once, what had happened?

"When they arrived, we lived in harmony. They exchanged their term of "fairy" and adopted our way of defining ourselves as "The People." We all lived companionably with the few native humans who traveled through our forest every few moon cycles, hunting the large beasts that once roamed this land. We lived in mutual respect. Then the situation changed."

"More humans found our forest and stayed. They settled, as we do, near water. They colonized very close to where the Fayes dwell now." Raine sipped another dew drop. "These humans traveled from the same place across the big river as the Fayes. Luckily, the humans did not know of the tails. Queen Tania's removal of all tails prevented a hunt even if the humans had known. However, from their own lore, these humans knew the habits of the Fayes, the relationship, and they honored it. For example, food was left out at night for the Fayes, and they no longer enjoyed the pleasure of supplying their own food. Queen Tania proclaimed the task menial and looked down at the Naturals for finding pleasure in the earth, preferring to live among man-made stone with small areas of forest."

Blaezi shuddered. She knew he was speaking of her and those like her. And he was right about their attitude. Hers wasn't exactly that way anymore, though, and she grew miffed at the old Natural for not noticing her attitude change.

"The Fayes feared these new humans might learn of the Glamour of the tail, so they removed them. Even if we weren't as drastic as the Fayes, all fairy troupes took measures to protect ourselves. The Moonbeam Ceremony for newborns was created at this time to insure that only natural humans could identify us easily. Other humans are confounded by the charm placed on our babies during the ceremony. Most humans confuse us with other forest creatures: lightning bugs, whippoorwills, hummingbirds—even lizards." Raine chuckled.

A small Natural, hearing the story for the first time, asked, "Fayes don't have tails?"

Raine shook his head. "Yes, little one. Of course, they *grow* tails. They do not, however, keep them. Their queen has their tails trimmed several times during each moon cycle and portions out their Glamour according to her whim. It is a very un-Natural thing to do, but," Raine looked sad, "she is trying to protect her People. More contact with humans than earth is bound to foster a bit of cruelty."

Tears filled Blaezi's eyes. Her wings tingled. She knew he was telling the truth, but she didn't want to remember that she was a part of it. She was, after all, a Faye. She did not, after all, have a tail.

"The Fayes changed with the humans, and our ways became so different that we almost completely severed ties—until now." Blaezi felt the eyes of a forest full of the Naturals and other creatures that had stopped along their way for an evening drink to hear a story. "The Fayes have adapted and now we need to know what they've learned. In a way, we are lucky that history has prepared the Fayes for us. If not, we would not have Blaezi to help us. Since she is a Garden Guard, she has had more contact with the earth than most." His wrinkles formed a smile then, and she loved him for what he said next. "This is why many of you have not found her so foreign. It's almost as if she belongs here."

The small Natural, crouching at Raine's feet spoke up again. "I saw Blaezi fall in the river and when she came out she said something about losing 'her portions.' She was talking about her Glamour, right?"

"You are wise, little one."

The small wings blushed at the praise, but he was still curious. "If she lost the Glamour she was given and she had no tail, how was she able to fly and seem healthy?"

"Little one, "Raine lifted the child into the air and laughed, "Glamour is power. The tail holds our Glamour." He cuddled the child in his arms. "But the strongest Glamour comes from within."

Blaezi's head rose higher and her wings became perkier than they had been at the beginning of Raine's story. *She held Glamour.* She held power. She would help the Naturals coexist with the humans—somehow. She would rescue the captives.

If anyone could accomplish Queen Tania's challenge, she could. And she would. Then she could return to the Fayes. Almost imperceptibly, Blaezi's wings sank. But would she want to?

CHAPTER 23

Blaezi yawned and crawled into her log for a good sleep. Just when she'd found a soft area of moss to lay her head, she heard a rustle.

A voice whispered, "Blaezi?"

Caution perked her wings as she edged toward the sound. A Faye couldn't be too careful with humans around.

"Blaezi!"

She saw Thorne and jumped at him. He yelped but recovered quickly. Blaezi mocked him in the light of the full moon.

"Looking for me?"

He stared at her, but when she thought he was about to turn and leave, he took a deep breath and sighed. "Yes. I needed to tell you something."

After Raine's story, the difficult day had become wonderful for Blaezi. The Naturals embraced her. She hadn't seen one glimpse of Rock so she figured he must have avoided her, and she hadn't missed his nasty comments that made others laugh. She grinned at the thought of his absence. Now Thorne looked like he was going to mess it all up again—unless he was going to apologize. Yep. That must be it.

"Go on, Thorne. Tell me what you need to say. It must be important if you waited until now."

"I didn't know until now." He moved closer to her and spoke

in a whisper. "I've noticed something about you." He paused. The moon glistened, silver in his hair. "You're different from the others, but you and I have something in common."

"Oh?"

"I noticed it tonight at the festival. You've got it. You've got your tail."

"I have a tail?"

Blaezi was afraid to look. She didn't want to be disappointed with something that resembled Rock's tail—or worse. When she looked over her shoulder, though, she could see a fully grown tail. She was impressed.

It was magnificent.

Long jagged strands of orange, yellow, and red seemed to dance with smooth flowing strands of the same colors. She caught her breath and said, "I've got a tail." Her eyes filled with tears and she looked at Thorne. "Thank you for telling me. Everyone else must have seen it, but I didn't know." She socked him. "You're not so bad."

He rubbed his shoulder and said, "Like a lot of personal changes, others often notice them first."

"Is that so?" She fluttered her wings. "Have you noticed anything else?"

"I have," he said. "Other than my own, I've rarely seen a tail grow that fast. Every other Natural takes several moons to grow. You've been here one moon cycle, and yours is fully developed."

"I hadn't thought about it," she said, "but I always had to trim mine more often than the other Fayes. I used to hate that about me." Blaezi pranced around and stared at her tail. "Not anymore."

Thorne laughed. Then he became serious. "Blaezi, I've got something else to say." Great. Finally! A real apology from this moody Natural. He'd been such a snit to her. She had to admit, though, that at other times, he was worth all of his moodiness. His shoulders tensed and he bowed his head. Guilt seeped in as she realized what Thorne was trying to tell her: Since Glamour came from tails, she should have shared some of her Glamour with the injured Naturals.

Instead, Thorne said, "When I thought you had skipped out on work to go to festival, I spent some time with Rock."

Remorse drained from her and Blaezi's eyes hardened. "Why wouldn't you? He's your friend. Oh, and he never liked me, so who could possibly be a better pal to listen to your complaints?"

"You're right." His wings dropped as he muttered, "I'm sorry."

"Eh?" Blaezi cupped her hand to her ear. "I don't think I heard you."

"You heard me. Now let me tell you the rest."

Blaezi didn't know it could get worse than Thorne telling Rock all about her faults.

Thorne said, "I told Rock I was going to follow you to see if you tried to connect with the human. I'm glad now that I did go because I was able to help the captives. Anyway, I think Rock went, too."

"So what?"

"So... he wasn't at the festival tonight." Blaezi tossed her hair over one shoulder. "Well, that explains why I had such a good time."

"No, Blaezi, you don't understand. I think she got him. I think he followed me because he thought it would be a funny show. He'd be able to tell first-hand stories of your failure at dinner." He looked at his hands. "Instead, he was captured."

"How do you know?"

"Have you seen the guy? He never misses a meal."

"What do you want me to do about it?"

Thorne said, "That's up to you. I know you have your own terms to deal with, but I'm going to let you know what I'm planning."

She waited.

"I'm going to get him and bring the others back, too."

Panic gripped her stomach. "You're right," she said. "I've got my own terms to deal with."

Thorne shook his head. "I thought you'd help. Don't you have any friends you've known for as long as your memories? They're Rock, Dogwood, and Laurel to me. I thought maybe you'd understand and help." He sat down and put his head in his hands. He seemed tired. "If Rock was captured, it's because I lured him there."

Blaezi thought about Diana and Dion. If they were captured, she'd try to save them—even if they hadn't tried to visit her. Besides, if the People were hunted for their tails in the past then they could be again. Perhaps by stopping it now she *would* be saving her friends.

"Remember what your terms are, Blaezi. You're supposed to help the Naturals with their problem. Well, if we've got a problem, this is it."

Blaezi looked up at the bright moon. The last time it was full she'd been home.

CHAPTER 24

In a hallway of Forrester High, Kat leaned against the wall before class started. Duncan stood with his arm resting on the wall close to her. A classmate, her brown hair pulled back in a ponytail, approached them with springy steps. Short cotton shorts revealed athletic, tan legs. She had perfect white teeth and a slight overbite. Her eyes, a deep brown, were wide when she smiled in an easy way.

"Hi, Duncan. Hi, Kat," she sang. She spoke to Duncan, "We've been in this class all summer, and here it is with our finals due next week and I've not even introduced myself. I feel just horrible since we'll be spending so many evenings together soon." Duncan raised an eyebrow, but she just smiled and winked at Kat. She focused attention on Duncan again, not that it had ever truly been diverted. "See, my brother's on the team, so I'll be cheering you on to victory when the season starts. It's going to be great." She waggled her spirit fingers at him. "Yea!"

"You're a cheerleader?" Duncan asked.

She shook her head. "Nope. I'm too busy playing soccer." She shrugged. "My brother and I try to make it to each other's games. So far, it's worked. Neither of our teams ever lost a game the other's watched."

Duncan said, "You want to tell me your name so I'll know who to thank?"

"Oh!" she blushed and her nose turned pink. "My name is Bernice—my parents named me after my grandmother—but my friends all call me Bunny. Right, Kat?"

Kat looked at her. She'd known this girl since elementary school. They'd been in Blue Birds together. She'd attended her first slumber party with her, but during middle school their friendship drifted. They'd always been on friendly terms, and she'd never before seen Bunny gush. Especially in a guy's direction. Usually, boys gushed at her. Of course, maybe she was just being friendly.

"Right, Kat?" Bunny repeated and examined Kat with a funny expression on her face.

"Um, yeah."

Bunny blinked her eyes at Duncan, her long lashes touching the top of her apple cheeks. "Duncan, I hope you don't mind, but I really need to borrow your... girlfriend?"

Duncan grinned at Kat. Their eyes met. So it was decided. They were boyfriend/girlfriend. Good. He pushed away from the wall, bent down, and picked his books from the floor.

"No problem." Duncan told Bunny. "Just be sure you give her back."

She batted her eyes at him and sniffed. "Don't be silly!"

Duncan pecked Kat on the cheek very near her lips. Both girls watched Duncan glide into the classroom, easily maneuvering through desks and people until he reached a group of guys who were already waiting for him at his desk.

Kat turned her attention to Bunny before Bunny's eyes had left Duncan.

"What's up?" asked Kat, trying to sound like she didn't mind other girls ogling her... boyfriend.

Bunny, alert again, reached for Kat's hands. "Oooh, Kat,

you've just *got* to tell me. *What* are you doing lately?"

Kat's body tensed. Could the girl know? Had she seen her in the woods? Had she watched her through her bedroom window? Kat made a mental note to shut the blinds from now on. Then Kat tried to relax. "What do you mean, Bunny?"

"Kat, everyone is talking about you!" She lifted her arms, Kat's hands in her own, and surveyed Kat. "Girl, you look amazing!"

Kat wanted to get her hands back but didn't want to be rude. Not with Bunny so eager to compliment her. "What are you talking about?"

Bunny released Kat's hands because she needed her own to speak properly. She was one of those people who talked with her entire body. "Honey, you can not hold out on me. We've known each other for, like, forever." She quickly walked around her, looking Kat up and down. "It's not that you've bought a whole new wardrobe.... It's not that you're fixing your hair differently...." Bunny stood still and asked, "So what is it? What's your beauty secret?"

Kat smiled. "If it's a secret, what makes you think I'll reveal it?"

"I hear you." Bunny nodded. "Okay, then, if you won't tell, will you share?"

Kat didn't know what she meant.

Bunny jumped right in. "Will you fix me up for the photo spread?"

Each year one of Forrester High's teams, clubs, or organizations modeled for the back-to-school photo spread of a local trendy clothing shop, Eden. Sometimes they even put a few commercials on television. This year's featured models were the soccer players.

"Pl-eeease," begged Bunny. "I just know you can make me look great! You've got a real gift for beauty."

What could Kat say to that?

CHAPTER 25

Over the next few days, life changed little among the Naturals. Many stayed away from the creek altogether. They remained cautious at the river. Aside from avoiding the human hunter, however, their lives continued as normal. They loved games and food and sought both. Even the liberated Naturals began to act as if nothing had happened. Laurel wasn't completely himself without his tail, but it had started to sprout again and he perked up. Above all, someone had to create new games!

Thorne and Blaezi knew something had happened, though. And they knew work still lay ahead.

"What's our plan?" Thorne asked her.

"I don't know yet."

Thorne nudged her. "You better figure it out soon. We're all depending on you."

Ever since Raine gave his speech, the Naturals treated her differently. They respected her, a feeling she'd never known. She had to help them. They needed her. And a small group of Naturals, including Rock, needed her more.

Of course, she'd be content to let the human do whatever she liked to Rock. Blaezi had her own fantasies. Perhaps the human pulled off his wings. Perhaps she removed each part of his tail one by one. Blaezi grinned, then shook it off. Rock was still one of the

People and even he didn't deserve that.

"I know," she said, "we've got to do something." She curled her knees under her chin and wrapped her hands around her ankles. "All right, you brought me here because you thought a Faye way could help. Let's use a Faye idea then."

"I'm listening," said Thorne.

She took a deep breath before letting it out slowly. "Fayes and humans have agreements. We guard their gardens and they let us eat as much as we want. According to lore, a similar agreement has gone on for many seasons: humans leave out food and we, in exchange, don't pull tricks on them."

Thorne said, "But we don't pull tricks on them. We stay out of their way."

"Not anymore." The plan was clearly developing in Blaezi's mind, so she spoke quickly. "We'll meet with the humans and inform them we're going to carry on this tradition. We're at an advantage since many humans aren't familiar with us. They don't know our limitations. Let them know what they need to know: what we like to eat and that they shouldn't mess with us. Avoid the human as much as possible, and we'll be okay."

Thorne nodded. "We should only approach humans who are as natural as possible."

"Yes. There have to be some left."

Thorne's wings grew dark as he asked, "What if we can't find one?" He looked at her, his mouth a firm line. "What if we run into the fairy hunter first?"

"We'll make her the offer."

"She knows about our tails, Blaezi! It's not that simple."

"Yes, it is. If we run into her first, we'll just have to sacrifice more." She narrowed her eyes. "We know the People can survive. Fayes have been doing it for as long as I've known."

"You don't mean...?"

Blaezi stuck her chin in the air. "Of course I do. We'll offer portions of Glamour in exchange for food. She'd be a ditzle not to take our offer."

"But Blaezi... what if she wants... more?"

"We'll just hope to find another human first. If we have to deal with her, we will. How are the rescue plans going?"

Thorne leaned back on his elbows. "Dogwood seems to have that well under control. He and Laurel have been working together to make it seem fun and enlist more Naturals to help."

"Good idea. When do we go?"

"During the waxing gibbous."

Blaezi looked at the sky then closed her eyes. The moon was partially dark. She had to accomplish her tasks soon. A moon's age had passed, and she had less than another to go before being banished forever.

She hopped up and clapped her hands at Thorne. "What are you waiting for? We've got a lot of work to do. Don't be a snail. C'mon!"

CHAPTER 26

At the Sonic drive-in, Kat set her vanilla Coke in the cup holder of Duncan's Mustang. He devoured the final mouthful of burger. She liked to watch him move—his jaws as he chewed, the line of his nose, the dexterity of his fingers, his forearm across the steering wheel. They'd been talking about whether they should go to a movie or try the new rock-climbing place. Her mind wandered to other activities, so Kat decided to change the subject.

"When we were at the river, you mentioned something about Little People. Do you believe in them?"

There was an extended pause before Duncan replied.

"I don't know. . ." he took a long sip from his water, "yeah."

"How big are they?"

Duncan shrugged. "Never seen one. Some say about knee high."

Kat thought of the box on her vanity. "Could they be smaller?"

"I guess." He became fascinated with his steering wheel. "Look, Kat, I don't feel comfortable talking about this. I don't talk about it to just anyone."

Kat pouted. "But I'm not just anyone." She placed a hand on his thigh. "Just one more question. Please?"

Duncan swallowed. Kat asked, "How do you know they're real? I mean, it's not like you've seen one."

He adjusted in his seat to face her. "Kat, you like science. You've studied things under a microscope."

"That's what I'm saying."

"No, Kat, it's not." He tried again. "You've studied things under a microscope. You know sometimes stuff that's real is not always easily visible."

"Sure," Kat conceded, "and sometimes what you think you see isn't real at all."

"Have a little faith." He took another sip of his water. "Why are you so interested in all of this anyway?"

Kat flashed a smile, hoping she had no tater tot remains in her teeth. "I want to know everything about you."

"I'll tell you something you might not know about me." He extended his arm across the seat and cupped the back of her neck and cheek with his large hand. No wonder he was a good basketball player.

Kat nuzzled into his hand and tried her best to appear alluring.

"I think I like you," he whispered. "A lot."

As if bewitched, the corners of her mouth twitched into a sly smile. "I already knew that," she whispered back.

CHAPTER 27

Blaezi and Thorne hunted humans. They stayed up all day to find them and prowled during the dark hours instead of attending evening festivities. It was difficult work. Neither Blaezi nor Thorne wanted to enter a highly populated area of humans. Instead they searched the woods for lone fisherman, daydreamers, and campers. Unlike the human who hunted the People, Blaezi and Thorne had no intentions of harming humans. The Naturals needed their help.

On the rare occasions when they found humans, they encountered difficulties. For some reason—possibly residual enchantment from the protective Moonbeam Ceremony for babies of the People—most humans did not seem to see them. Even when one did, he shook his head and said he needed to get his eyes checked. Or she would say, "Did you see that?" and whoever was with her would say, "No. What?" And the first one would furrow her brow and squint her eyes and say, "Nothing. Never mind."

They found a fisherman sleeping one day and crawled onto his face. They danced on his nose in hopes of rousing him, but wound up resting on his cheeks until he finally opened his eyes. Blaezi and Thorne each sat on a cheek, staring at an eyelid until it fluttered open. When it did, his eyes grew very wide and his eyes crossed as he tried to focus on Blaezi and Thorne. He tightly shut his eyelids and muttered, "I must still be dreaming." And then drifted off into sleep again, his snores echoing down the riverbank.

One evening, the two heard pops and crackles and felt the warmth of a campfire even though the evening was hot. A group of male humans laughed and talked and made little sense at all. They threw cans into the fire and shot bottles with BB guns. Blaezi determined that humans in the Natural part of the world were much less desirable than those in the Faye world. Thorne tried to encourage her. "Maybe we just haven't met the right ones yet." She hoped so. They sneaked toward the ruckus. The rowdiest of the humans spoke to Blaezi and Thorne.

"Hi there, little fellers!" he cried. "You want a drink?"

The rest of his entourage laughed at their friend, bent talking to the ground.

Blaezi said, "Sir, I am Blaezi, a Faye. Do you have the desire to enter into negotiations with the Naturals?"

The man stood up straight and considered this. He was pleased to be spoken to with such respect—even if the creatures were tiny, they still looked very much like people. Blaezi had not heard this human's slurred dialect before. "Follow me to my office." He walked, rather clumsily, to a rock on the far side of the fire and plopped down. Blaezi and Thorne followed him. "I suppose I am interested in negotiations." He giggled, and then contorted his face into formal solemnity. "What do you want to," he took another swig of his beverage, "negotiate?"

His friends watched the man as he seemingly spoke to the ground before the fire. Occasionally, his head lolled around as if he were following a firefly zipping about in the air. He nodded in agreement several times. Finally, he called to his buddies and motioned them over. "C'mon over here, you girlie men!" He attempted a whisper but only succeeded in spewing spittle on Blaezi and Thorne. "Don't be afraid of these little people. They're not gonna hurt us. They need our help."

One of the women stood from her perch on the human transportation, a big metal wagon, and said, "He's drunk. I'm taking him home before he gives away our first born." The humans all laughed.

Blaezi translated to Thorne what she'd said. He replied, "That's not a bad idea to use as collateral."

Before they could discuss it with their new friend, his babbling body was dragged into the bed of the truck by his buddies and driven off by the woman. The remaining people didn't seem to pay them any attention—even though Blaezi and Thorne were pretty sure they saw them. They just kept saying, "Man, this is strong stuff," and took more sips from their cans.

CHAPTER 28

Poster boards lined the classroom walls. The elaborate nature of the ecosystems varied by degrees. One consisted of a fishbowl, a tri-fold screen, and a tape recorder. Another was a 45 minute video tape, filmed by the student. The most aromatic project was a miniature version of a student's bedroom, complete with pizza crust underneath the bed and smelly socks hanging from the doorknob. Other final projects were not so extensive. One was merely a piece of notebook paper with scribbled pictures completed during the last two minutes before the morning bell. Another just a piece of cardboard that the student claimed held an entire ecosystem no human could see with the naked eye. Each student waited for Coach Axe to pass judgment.

As was often the case, Axe didn't appear after the bell rang. Or even after ten minutes of class. The students investigated the projects themselves.

"Cool!" said one student. "Check this out!" Several students hustled to a corner where Kat's project rested.

She panicked. Had she mistakenly included one of her "chameleons"? She thought she had safely stored them all.

Duncan and Kat wandered over to check out the source of their awe. Duncan spoke first. "What's up?"

"Dude! Have you seen this?" The boy had reached inside the vivarium and pulled out a frog. "It don't have no tongue."

Duncan asked, "How can you tell?"

"I opened its mouth." He shoved it in Duncan's face.

"Why?" Kat asked.

The boy shrugged.

Duncan was speechless.

"La-di-da, aren't you girlie men all excited?"

Heads whirled in the direction of the voice. Coach Axe stood behind his desk wearing shorts, t-shirt, and sandals. He growled at the class. "What are you waiting for? Sit down while I try to figure out what's going on today." He rifled through his desk drawer until he located a bottle of aspirin and consumed several pills. Duncan and Kat exchanged looks.

The boy placed the frog in the relative safety of Kat's vivarium and returned to his desk.

A young man sitting by himself on the far left side of the classroom raised his trembling hand.

"Yeah, sugar britches?"

"Um... Mr... Coach... we were supposed to turn in our final projects today."

Axe pulled a yellow piece of torn paper from the top desk drawer. His eyes scanned the paper and he frowned. "You're right. I see that here on the... lesson plan." His frown deepened when he said, "Well, let's grade them so you can take it home to show your mommy for a cookie. Maybe she'll put it on the fridge."

The boy sulked while another student threw a paper airplane at him. Axe shook his head at the aspiring aerospace engineer who retrieved the paper from the floor and tossed it in the trashcan.

Axe crossed his arms and shoved his fingers under his biceps to make them look bigger. He walked toward the projects. "Let's see what we have here."

He asked questions about each one, proving he knew a lot

more than just dribbling and lay-ups. The last ecosystem was Kat's. "You have these labeled as ordinary frogs found in a creek near your house."

Kat nodded.

"Have you seen other frogs there without tongues?"

Kat answered truthfully. "Lots of them. Ever since I was a little girl."

Axe gripped his chin and whispered, "No kidding." Finally, he peeled his eyes from the frogs and looked at Kat.

"I don't know without looking it up, but I believe you may have them mislabeled."

Kat bit back her objection. She knew they were labeled correctly. What did this guy know anyway? She couldn't tell him why she knew they had no tongues, so she tried to think of something to avoid losing an A in the class.

Axe brought her to attention. "Kat's your name, right?"

Kat nodded.

"Well, don't worry about your grade." He peered through the glass again. "I wouldn't be surprised if you found a new species."

Kat tried not to smirk.

Coach Axe leaned against the teacher's desk and looked at the clock. "That took all of twenty minutes, and summer school lasts all day, doesn't it?"

A group of students joined in pleas for dismissal. They already had visions of doing nothing while other summer school students suffered through finals. Perhaps they could still get in a few hours of lazy summer before they had to report next week to get their schedules for the new school year.

Axe offered a pretend pout. "Ohhhhhh. I know. Life is so unfair. You probably want to float the river or go swimming or something rather than stay in a classroom when the work is all done. I know. I know. Life is soooo tough." He crossed his arms. "How about this...." He eyed the projects. "Those of you who had your general release forms signed by your parents or guardians get to go on a field trip. The rest of you can go home—or meet us with a signed release form at the river."

The class cheered.

"Really? We can go home?" a boy asked.

His buddy thumped him on the forehead. "No, dope. He said we're going to the river. We're gonna get in canoes and float the river."

Kat looked down at what she was wearing. There was no way that she wanted to ruin her outfit with river water. As usual, Duncan seemed to sense her emotions and raised his hand.

"Coach?"

"Yep?"

"Can we have some time so we can get our swimsuits?"

"How 'bout this?" He motioned to the projects. "Why don't you guys get rid of those things while we're at it? This will be a learning experience. Some of you can return your creatures to the wild. And some of you... who turned in blank poster board, for instance, might actually learn something from this class on a field trip." He examined his watch. "We'll meet at Rent 'Em Canoes in an hour. You guys and gals can bring ice chests and snacks if you want." He put on sunglasses and adjusted his cap. "Just remember. . . bring money and sunscreen, but NO glass containers and NO alcohol."

CHAPTER 29

Blaezi and Thorne staked out a busy area of the river where stones had been set up to see-saw.

Thorne bounced up. "Even though there are a lot of humans around here, they're bound to be more natural than those who stay in the human stone dwellings."

Blaezi hit the ground with a thud. "Maybe so, but *your* humans are not as good as our Faye humans." She shoved with her legs.

Thorne held the see-saw in the air with his Glamour and they hovered equidistance from the rocks below. "Why do you say things like that?"

Blaezi wiggled her legs to try to make the rock fall one way or the other. It didn't move. "Like what? I say the truth as I see it."

"Yeah, as you see it," he said. "You've been wrong before. Admit it. You like the Naturals better than the Fayes."

Blaezi took flight. The absence of her weight sent Thorne and his Glamour to the earth with a jolt. He scrambled to right himself as she spoke. "Sure. I like some Naturals better than some Fayes. *You* obviously wouldn't know *who* I liked."

Thorne said, "All I know is if you were my friend, I would have come to help you by now. You only have a few more nights left—"

"I know. I don't want to talk about my friends. What do you know about friendship anyway? You're just helping me so the

Naturals don't turn on you for bringing them a banished Faye."

"Maybe I was... but you're not so bad. I'd like to see you get what you want."

"Great," said Blaezi. "I want to stop talking about this." She narrowed her eyes. "Besides, I see some humans. A group of them are launching canoes."

***

Duncan and Kat loaded their canoe with an ice chest and sunscreen. They each wore baseball caps and grubby tennis shoes. Kat refused to ruin a pair of decent shoes, but her cap was new. Duncan coached a few classmates, who had never floated before, on the basics as Kat put on her life jacket over her tank top. Duncan had not grown up here but had often visited relatives and spent many summer days lazing along the river. Kat, who grew up near the river and spent time easing along it in a canoe or inner tube, knew the dangers of its deceptive appearance. They knew it looked calm, but the current could flip a boat over and drag a person under before anyone else even noticed. As Bunny approached, Kat tried to remember how many people had died the previous summer.

"Hi, Kat," she purred. "Everyone else seems to be full, so Coach told me to hitch a ride with you guys. Do you mind?"

Duncan clapped a hand on Kat's shoulder. "Hop on in. Got your life jacket?"

Bunny smiled at him. "Sure. I'm not wearing the silly old thing, though." She winked at Kat. "I'm wearing a new suit. If you guys are going to paddle, then I can get a tan." Just as Kat was thinking she could use some sun herself, Bunny peeled off her t-shirt and kicked off her shorts with the finesse of a stripper. Kat decided if she had breasts like Bunny's, she'd wear a bikini in public as often as possible. Since she did not, she tightened her life jacket and smiled at Duncan—who was still smiling at Bunny.

"I'll be right back. I forgot something," Kat said and moved toward the parking lot.

Duncan managed to stop staring at Bunny and focused his full attention on Kat. "Did you decide to free your ecosystem?"

"Nope," she smiled. "You heard Coach Axe. I need to investigate more. I may have discovered a new species." She whirled around and ran to the car. She pulled what appeared to be a makeup brush from her purse and dusted it across her face. She unfastened her jacket and brushed it across her chest, suit, and flat stomach. "Any little bit helps." She slammed the door of Duncan's Mustang and ran back to the canoes. She didn't want to leave them together too long. She didn't like the way Duncan looked at Bunny—for that matter, when Duncan was around, she just didn't like the way Bunny looked.

"What did you forget?" Bunny asked as she looked at Kat's empty hands.

"Oh... nothing! I forgot that I already put my water in the ice chest." Bunny laughed at her, and Duncan shook his head as he smiled a crooked smile.

Duncan whispered in her ear, "You're hot. Crazy, but hot."

Kat knew he'd say something like that.

Metal and fiberglass scraped against rocks as the class began launching their canoes. "Hustle, everyone!" Axe called. "It's time for a water adventure!"

Kat said, "Alright, let's go. Bunny, you sit in front, I'll sit in the middle, and Duncan can sit in the back."

Duncan said, "Um. I think Bunny should sit between us since you and I are paddling."

Kat batted her eyes at him.

"What?" he asked.

She smiled, waiting for the magic to take effect. It didn't.

"Kat, c'mon, they're leaving us. This is going to be so much fun!" Bunny grabbed Kat's hand and pulled her towards the canoe. "Let's talk about tomorrow's photo shoot."

"Fine," Kat said. "For starters, you should probably cover up. I'd really hate for you to get sunburned."

"Good thinking!" said Bunny as she put on her life jacket and slathered sunscreen on her face. "You're so thoughtful, Kat."

"Yeah, she is..." said Duncan as Kat removed her life jacket and t-shirt to reveal a bikini, "pretty spectacular."

Somehow, she knew he'd say something like that, too.

***

The canoes glided along the river. Periodically, Coach Axe pointed out bits of nature: "Boy, get back in your canoe! That's algae, not grass. It grows on the back waters in the dog days of summer." He also highlighted geographical points of interest, "That big rock up ahead is called Elephant's Head because the big rock is shaped like, well, an elephant's head with its trunk in the water." As the canoes approached an area where tree limbs reached out from the bank to the water, Axe called out, "Don't touch the branches!"

"Why?" asked Bunny.

"Because," said Kat with the experience of one who spent hours in the woods, "snakes like to sun themselves on the branches. If you reach for one, you might shake it into your boat."

Bunny squealed. Kat turned around to give her a look and locked eyes with Duncan who was easily maneuvering the canoe. He shook his head in a way that indicated Bunny was a dumb girl. Kat was relieved he thought Bunny was silly, but when his eyes returned to survey Bunny, Kat suspected he wasn't thinking of her brain power.

Bunny said, "Those poor snakes must be so scared when they

land in a boat full of people. I'd bite someone if I were them, too."

To Kat's dismay, Duncan said, "You've got a point. We're invading their environment. It's almost as if we get what we deserve if we don't respect them."

"True," retorted Kat. "If something jumped in my boat that didn't belong I might do all I could to hurt it if it didn't know its place."

"Well, I know my place," Bunny said, her eyes on the branches. "It's away from those trees." She grabbed the canoe paddle at her feet and whipped it out—barely missing Kat's head—and paddled with strong, deep strokes. The canoe drifted to a crooked position.

"Whoa!" cried Duncan. "You don't need to do that. I've got it back here." But it was too late.

The canoe entered a current and turned back to front downriver. Bunny squealed. The canoe rushed toward the embankment, a tall grey cliff of flint rock—the stuff from which American Indians of the past fashioned arrowheads. With a crash in its very near future, the canoe tunneled through the overhanging trees.

"Don't-hit-the-branches-don't-hit-the-branches," Bunny chanted as she skittered around in the canoe, avoiding dangling tree limbs.

Kat tried to stabilize the canoe but had a difficult time due to the current, the tree limbs, and Bunny's rocking. She looked at Duncan. He was paddling like a champion in an attempt to straighten their path.

Over his head, Kat saw two, tiny, human-like figures sitting on a thick branch. Her mouth flew open. They weren't on a branch. A ribbon of tongue lashed out and hissed in Kat's direction. She screamed. A water moccasin, ridden by a couple of tiny creatures, flopped into their canoe. Bunny shrieked and jumped into the river, upsetting the canoe and taking the remaining passengers with her.

***

Blaezi and Thorne were taken by surprise when they saw the fairy hunter in the canoe. Blaezi's body twitched when she recognized her, and the snake, mistaking her movement, flopped off the branch. They realized the other humans were scared, so they flew off the snake and let it slide into the safety of the water and glide away.

Thorne said, "Those two don't seem to be like her."

Blaezi watched all of them react to the water and try to find shore. She had to agree.

"Don't the natural humans spend a day on the river for fun?" asked Blaezi. Thorne nodded in response and continued to watch the fairy hunter as she attempted to come up for air. "Then why is *she* here? Is she scouting for more of us?" Blaezi's wings stilled. "If so, she knows we're here. She'll come for us." She reached out and grabbed Thorne's hand. When she realized what she'd done, she released it. "I don't get it. If she likes nature, why does she hunt us? I mean, I understand why some humans hunt animals—they eat them and it keeps animals from starving to death in the woods due to overpopulation."

"I guess just because you like something doesn't mean you protect it," said Thorne.

Blaezi thought of Dion and Diana; she'd try to protect them even if they weren't helping her.

Thorne watched the human reach shore, and then he looked at Blaezi grimly. "Who knows? Maybe we do need to be hunted." Before Blaezi could react he said, "With so much human construction happening in our forest, if we don't find help soon, we might become overpopulated for our food sources, too."

Blaezi's eyes filled with tears and her wings tingled. "We won't be hunted for food or clothes—but for our tails."

CHAPTER 30

The first time Kat surfaced, her head hit the top of the overturned canoe. She was able to get a deep breath before she went under again. She swam hard upriver in hopes the canoe would be carried away from her. The next time she tried to surface, she felt the scraping of the tree limbs as well as the pressure of a nearby overturned log sucking her under. The third time she tried to surface, she managed to reach open air. She felt an arm grip her and pull her toward shore. It was one of the students from a nearby canoe who had seen them tip. The other passengers retrieved their canoe with one paddle and pulled it alongside her before returning to their own.

"You gonna be okay?" he asked.

"Sure. Go on," she said. Fear gripped her stomach as she reached for her rescuer's wrist and asked, "Where's Duncan?"

The boy pointed. "Isn't he your boyfriend?"

Kat swallowed and nodded. She closed her eyes and almost said a prayer of thanks.

The boy shrugged and his buddy pushed their canoe into the water before hopping in. They called out, "See ya, Duncan" and "Looks like you've got your hands full!"

Kat whirled her head in the direction of their calls. Walking up the rocky shore was Duncan. In his arms, he cradled Bunny. Her arms were wrapped around his neck, and her head was snuggled

GLAMOUR

into his shoulder. He said something to her and they both laughed. She craned her neck and... oh no she didn't!

Yes, she did!

Bunny pecked him on the cheek. He, of course, grinned from ear to ear. Then he saw Kat.

He set Bunny on a large stone a little ways downriver and said something to her. Then he approached Kat, who stood with her hands on her hips.

He put both hands on her shoulders and squeezed. Looking into her eyes, he said, "How ya doin'?"

Kat's eyes flickered. "Well, I don't much like being thrown into water by a girl freaking out for no good reason, but I managed to land on my feet."

Duncan jerked his head back. "No good reason? Kat! A snake was in our boat."

"Yeah," she said as her eyes slid over to Bunny, "I know."

"It landed in her lap!"

"If she wouldn't have touched the branches when freaking out, we wouldn't have had that problem."

"Kat, don't be like this. She didn't touch the branches. The canoe bumped into them. The snake just seemed to leap off the branch."

Kat remembered what she had seen on top of the snake and changed the subject. She lowered her chin and looked up at him. "Why didn't you help *me*? I'm your girlfriend. Why didn't you try to save me instead of her?"

He looked at Bunny who had removed her sopping life jacket and was, once again, displaying all her glory in the tiny bikini as she reclined on a big rock, soaking up the sun. "You seem to be able to take care of yourself."

"Really?" said Kat. "I was the one without a life jacket!" She stormed over to Bunny and kicked some pebbles. "Let's go. We've got to catch up with the others."

"Did you see them, Kat? Did you see what I saw on that snake?" asked Bunny.

Kat paused mid-stride toward the canoe and turned around. "What do you mean?"

"There were little creatures. They looked like... like...."

Kat interrupted. "Chameleons. Yeah. I saw them. They look like the chameleons that I'd started to use in my ecosystem. Let's go."

"No," Bunny persisted. "They looked like people."

Chameleons? People? *Little* people? Kat's mind worked overtime. Why hadn't she seen this before?

They heard rocks crunch, and Duncan was beside them. "Duncan saw them, too, but he doesn't want to talk about it." Bunny smiled at him and reached over and squeezed his arm. As soon as she touched him, he flexed. Kat performed a mental eye roll. "That's okay. If he's going to save me, then he doesn't have to talk about it if he doesn't want to." She said to Kat, "You are soooo lucky, Kat. If he were my boyfriend I wouldn't let other girls near him. I swear I wouldn't!"

Kat said sweetly, "Well, it's a good thing you don't have to worry about that." She looked at Duncan who was still smiling at Bunny. "Besides, you want to know why he doesn't want to talk about the creatures?" She thought about it for a moment before continuing. She didn't want to expose what she suspected to be true of these creatures' existence, but she didn't think it would hurt around Bunny. Moreover, Duncan needed something to shift his attention. "Duncan thinks they're his Little People!" She forced a laugh. "He probably thinks they tipped us over on purpose." She nodded in mock seriousness. "You know, he thinks the Little

People do that to humans sometimes."

Duncan looked at Kat with hurt in his eyes. Then an expression she'd never seen from him flitted across his face: anger. She almost felt guilty. Almost.

Bunny said, "You never know."

"What?" Kat mocked. "Do you believe in them?"

"I don't know, but I've heard a story or two."

"Do tell."

Duncan reached for the life jacket on the rocks and said, "We need to get going."

Kat linked her arm in Bunny's. "And Bunny, you can tell us a couple of stories while we're catching up with the others."

Back in the canoe, Duncan paddled to catch up with the rest of the class. With constant prompting from Kat, Bunny told stories. Duncan scanned the trees and water for more hazards.

"Isn't that right, Duncan?" asked Bunny.

His attention was pulled to the girls.

"Didn't they used to think the Little People only protected Cherokees?"

Duncan shrugged and reverted to scanning the river.

"Well, that's what people thought. They protect all people, though, even those as white as you!" Bunny laughed. Kat's skin *was* fair, but she didn't look ill. On the contrary, she thought she resembled Cinderella. Kat looked down at Bunny's arm, dark from hours outside. Kat could be that tan, but she wore sunscreen daily. She smiled. Not at Bunny's joke—but at picturing Bunny's future sun damaged skin.

Finally, Duncan spoke to them. "How do you know so much?"

"I pay attention, silly. I've grown up here, remember? If you just listen, you hear lots. Like, I know about the Little People protecting everyone because I used to baby sit for these friends of the family who lived in the country. Sometimes the old grandfather would stick around while I was there, and he'd talk and talk. He talked about a time he'd wandered into the woods when he was only a couple of years old. His family looked for him. Friends and neighbors looked for him, but after a while, they just figured he'd been eaten by a bobcat or something. They were planning the funeral when, a few days later, he showed up. He wore the same clothes he had on when he disappeared, and they were clean. He was clean and he'd been fed. They all decided the Little People had taken care of him even though his father wasn't Cherokee—he was some white dude from Kentucky."

"Did he tell you what they looked like?" asked Kat.

"He didn't remember exactly. Besides, most people have never seen them."

"Yeah, that's what Duncan said."

The girls looked at him for a response, but he remained as silent as a tree.

Bunny continued, "His description doesn't match what I saw today, though. They had tails."

Duncan stopped paddling and leaned forward. He asked Bunny the question, but he looked at Kat. "Did you say tails?"

"Yeah, it was so cool—whatever they were. And I can see why Kat thought they were chameleons at first. They blended in almost perfectly with the tree and the snake. Didn't they, Kat?"

Kat nodded. She wanted to know more. Duncan had said that she should respect them, but he never said why they deserved it. "Since Duncan's not talking... why do you think he's so quiet about them?"

Bunny said, "I don't know." She turned and looked at Duncan who was still searching the landscape and paddling. "Duncan, do you want us to stop? I don't mean to be insensitive. Is this bothering you?"

He breathed in the clean air and let it out. "Nah. That's okay." He glared at Kat. "Thank you for asking, though. I've just never spoken about it much outside of my family. My grandmother told me a lot of people think of it as superstitious and anti-Christian. Not the best combination in the Bible Belt."

"It *is* superstitious!" said Kat with a laugh. "Do you believe in voodoo, too?"

"No, it's not," cried Bunny. "Do you think believing in water is superstitious?" She dipped her fingers in the river and playfully flicked Kat with water. "You see it. It's there. You feel it. It's there. Well, you saw those Little People today. I know you did. You even said you almost put them in your ecosystem. You talked about them in class, but you called them chameleons. That's not superstition; it's mistaken identity."

Kat said, "Duncan's never seen them."

"Yeah, but I still respect that they might be there," he said.

"Why?" Kat asked.

Duncan paused in his rhythmic paddling. "Bunny told a story. Now I'll tell a story." He let the canoe float with the guidance of the water, slipping the paddle in every once in a while to prevent them from getting too close to shore. "When I was little, we were supposed to go to Disney World. My grandmother came with us. When we returned, we took her home." He paused and shook his head. "Grandma was so upset. Every single piece of pottery in her house had been broken. Everything else was undisturbed. She was frightened, but mostly she was angry at herself."

"Why? Did she leave the doors unlocked?" Kat asked. "She might have been getting her picture taken with Mickey Mouse when some neighborhood vandals broke in."

Duncan shook his head. "There was no sign of breaking and entering, and I locked the doors myself. She said she hadn't left any food out for the Little People. She claimed they were hungry, and she had neglected them when she left. She always used to leave food on her back porch. I remember taking it out there when I was a little boy." He grinned the way people do when they remember Santa and the Tooth Fairy. "Anyway, she was so excited to go on the trip with us she forgot to leave out food."

Bunny was enthralled. "So, they just came in and tore up her stuff?"

"Yeah, but that was the last time."

"I guess she always left food out for them after that?" asked Kat.

"She sure did. Lots of it. Also, she had my dad build her a little barbed wire fence around her back porch. It was only about ankle high. He even made a little gate for it. Whenever she was home, she left the gate open. Whenever she left, though, she closed the gate to keep them out and to let them know she was gone."

CHAPTER 31

Plans were underway. Dogwood bound blades of grass together to make rope. Thorne wrapped some of the finished rope around a twig, attaching a hollowed out half of a walnut hull. Blaezi sharpened swords she'd fashioned from a nearby thorn tree. Laurel waited for the Naturals to return with supplies. True to his nature, he'd made it a game, so they were racing to retrieve the most sweet gum balls, the round, prickly fruit of a tree.

"Don't you think it's strange we haven't had any more hunter sightings?" asked Blaezi.

A shiver ran over Laurel, and his wings paled. "Not really. She managed to capture almost everyone who saw her."

Dogwood's movements became fierce as he made the rope. "Well, we won't have to worry about her much longer. We'll bring our Naturals home."

Laurel said, "Do you think something has already happened? She hasn't taken anyone since Rock."

Blaezi giggled. "Well, he would be enough to make me change my mind! Maybe *he's* done something to *her*."

"We can hope," said Thorne. He attached his work to a larger contraption that had taken much longer to produce.

Laurel jumped up in excitement. "They're coming!" Before following his gaze, the others exchanged happy glances. Laurel was becoming more like himself these days. Then they looked in the direction of the approaching Naturals.

Laurel offered commentary on the sport he'd created. "Rose Rock is on the outside carrying what appears to be a rather sharp sweet gum ball. Yes, folks, you can see her wince in pain as Lichen knocks against her before he takes the lead. Others are back there, but these two are going to fly it out to see who's first."

Blaezi, Thorne, and Dogwood dropped their work to cheer on the rivals. Dogwood congratulated all the Naturals as they flew in and deposited their porcupine spheres next to Thorne. Laurel started telling them about his next "game"—rattlesnake lassoing.

Before the competitors flew to the new event, they wanted to see Thorne's catapult work. Thorne tugged on the rope that pulled the walnut hull down to the ground. Made from a soft wood, the twig bent. Dogwood placed a sweet gum ball in the walnut hull. When Thorne let go of the rope, the sweet gum ball flew through the air. The crowd cheered.

"When we get those sharpened, they'll be perfect," said Thorne.

CHAPTER 32

The day had not gone as Kat planned. Duncan offered to take Bunny home, and he dropped Kat off first. She needed to see Duncan to smooth things over. More importantly, she needed him to see her. Before sitting at the computer she fed the creatures— were they the Little People Duncan spoke of? Nevertheless, she made sure she covered her fingertips with their magic. She could use all the help she could get. She was relieved to see he was online even though it was marked as "Away." He didn't seem like the sort of person who screens messages. She looked at her fingers, took a deep breath, and typed.

Kiddykat: F2T?

Duncan didn't respond, so Kat assumed that he must be away from the computer. Still, she figured that she might as well mend as much as she could.

Kiddykat: I'm sorry.

Kat paused. She'd rarely spoken those words, much less written them. They looked odd to her. Had she spelled them correctly? However, she knew she should use them in order to keep Duncan. Also, if her creatures were Little People, she needed his knowledge. He could read her message later.

Kiddykat: Really. I'm sorry. I shouldn't have been so upset about Bunny getting in our canoe. I just wanted time alone with you. And I really shouldn't have brought up your Little People. I wasn't making fun of you.
Hawk: yes you were

The response was quick and the *bling*-ing sound that the computer made when the message appeared might as well have been a slap. Maybe he *was* screening messages: hers.

She was fast on her feet, though, and caught herself.

Kiddykat: I shouldn't have. I'm sorry. I won't do it again.

Duncan didn't respond.

Kiddykat: Can we meet somewhere and talk about this?

He waited so long to respond that she was contriving another message when her computer *blinged* at her.

Hawk: I've got early practice

Kat looked at the clock in the bottom corner of her screen. It was only 4:00.

Kiddykat: That's okay. I understand. I've got an early morning, too. I just want to make everything right between us.
Hawk: forget about it

Kat felt more relieved than when she was a little girl and watched the dermatologist burn off her warts. Ugly things can go away quickly when handled right.

Hawk: I was IMing a friend earlier who told me how lucky I was to have you as a girlfriend

She smiled and couldn't help herself from wondering who thought she was so great. Her mind played back the guys in the zo class who sat by her and Duncan. In her music video brain, they sighed and gazed longingly at her as she studiously answered all of the questions at the end of the book. When she dropped her pencil, they offered her theirs in perfect tempo with the music.

Kiddykat: Who?

Hawk: Bunny

Oh.

Kiddykat: I'd love to know more about it, but I have to go.

Hawk: getting ready for tomorrow?

Kiddykat: Yeah. It's the photo shoot, and I'm doing Bunny's makeup.

Hawk: sounds like an easy job. she looks pretty good already

Kat bit the inside of her mouth when she clenched her teeth together. In her video mind, the boys who worshiped her a moment earlier now doted on Bunny.

Kiddykat: Definitely. Especially if you like that natural, home-grown look.

Hawk: whoa! no need for the claws. another

guy might think you were jealous
Kiddykat: I never get jealous.

No. She got even. However, she would make Bunny more beautiful tomorrow. She couldn't help herself. She loved making the world a prettier place.

Hawk: have fun
Kiddykat: I definitely will. I'll see you later.
Hawk: after the shoot?
Kiddykat: Sure. You can pick me up there. I'll call you when it's over.
Hawk: later

Kat walked to her closet and pulled out her travel makeup holder. She'd purchased new makeup since Bunny asked her to do the shoot. She wanted to do a good job. What if the photographer noticed her? What if he asked her to model? What if he asked her to work all of his shoots? She carefully packed all of the new makeup.

She opened a small compact, placed it on the vanity, and lifted the box that held the creatures. Cracking the lid a tiny slit, she shook it like mad. Except for the faint, sparkly dust falling out of the slit and landing in the compact, anyone watching might think she was trying to guess what was inside it. Anyone listening might think she was playing heavy maracas with all of the thumping the creatures made against the walls of the box. They hardly screamed at all anymore.

Tomorrow morning she would pack a few of the creatures' tails. She might even break off a new one to ensure freshness.

She pulled one from the holder and brushed it across her cheeks. She smiled at the results in the mirror. Tomorrow would be a beautiful day!

CHAPTER 33

Journal Entry

I could never have dreamed what happened today. The photo shoot was great. Since Bunny was so determined to show off her body yesterday, she got sunburned. I was able to fix that though and make her naturally ordinary self look extraordinary. The other soccer girls had me do their makeup, too. The photographer liked my work I could tell. After all, he saw what I had to work with when they walked in.

Bunny looked so great her mom hired me on the spot! (Her mom is a field reporter on the news. She does special segments like standing by the highway when a tornado is coming or talking to the neighbors about a person going to court because of some stupid crime.) Anyway, while we were talking about it, she got a phone call. They needed her to report to work right away and she wanted me to go with her. (Bunny was so jealous because when she asked her mom for a ride home, she grabbed me and we took off. She told Bunny to get another ride. She even bought me a snack at the 7-11 down the street.)

Her interview made all the national networks! Almost all of them made remarks about how pretty she was. One lady on CNN even commented about who did her makeup, but she didn't know she was on the air. Mrs. Herrald got a promotion! Just like that. She starts on the evening news tomorrow night. She asked me to be on their "Teen Focus" segment as her first interview. I can't wait.

Kat closed her journal and placed it in its spot beside her book of fairy tales. She had just turned off the light and closed her eyes when they immediately popped open again. Duncan! She had told him she'd call him to pick her up after the photo shoot.

After tearing back the covers, she leapt from bed and raced toward her cell phone. She had turned off the ringer before she left the house so it wouldn't interrupt the shoot, and with all of the excitement never bothered to check it. Five messages.

"First message" the electronic voice on the phone chanted at her.

"Hi." It was Duncan. "Just calling to wish you good luck. Hope everything goes 'beautifully perfect' for you today. Talk to you later."

"Seven thirty a.m." the phone chanted. Kat smiled and felt as if the starlight shining through her window warmed her. He'd definitely forgiven her. She didn't delete it because she might want to listen to it later.

"Second message."

"Sister." It was her mom. Since her mother had been raised in Oklahoma, she kept with the southern term of endearment. Kat's mind wandered to why men called their sons and anyone else's son "son," but women called their daughters "sister." She had missed most of the message when she finally paid attention. "So, we'll just see you late tonight or in the early morning." Kat pressed the seven on the phone pad to delete the message.

"Three thirty p.m."

"Third message."

"Kat?" It was Duncan again. "Um... I hope everything's okay. I'm looking forward to seeing you. Give me a call."

"Four forty-five p.m."

"Fourth message."

"Thank you!!!" A chorus of soccer players yelled at her through the phone before erupting into giggles. She moved it a little from her ear and winced. A single, enthusiastic voice came through the line. "Kat, this is Emily." Kat smiled as she reflected on how pretty Emily had looked after she finished with her. Emily was a decent person who used her brain, but her propensity for bad hair days usually overshadowed her good qualities. Kat had remedied that flaw. "We just wanted to thank you for helping us look so good. If you finish up with Mrs. Herrald's makeup soon, we're hanging out at my house. You and Bunny should drop by. I live at 739..." Her voice trailed off as Kat looked at the clock and deleted the message. She wondered why Emily assumed Bunny was with her. "Six twelve p.m."

"Fifth message."

Duncan's voice sounded calmer than his last message. "I hope you had a great day, Kat. I guess you got another ride home. I look forward to hearing all about it. Sorry I've left you so many messages today."

"Eight thirty-three p.m."

Kat felt a pang of an emotion to which she was unaccustomed. Was it guilt? She attempted to rid herself of it. Duncan would have known she got busy, right? He could have called her house and spoken to her parents. Kat remembered her parents were gone. Duncan must have been worried about her. Guilt came back stronger. She had told him she'd call him, but she'd just forgotten all about it... and him. How could that happen? She dialed his number.

A sleepy voice answered the phone. "Hmmm?"

"Duncan?"

"Umhmmm."

"This is Kat. Did I wake you?"

"Umhumm. Ugh. Uh-uh." She heard movement, probably

him sitting up in bed. She wondered if he slept in pajamas or just shorts or... . He cleared his throat. "No."

"Oh, good," she said. "Listen, lots of crazy things happened today and I should have called you, but I didn't." Her voice grew sweet and she batted her eyelashes even though he wasn't there to witness the affect. "Forgive me?"

She thought she sensed him smile on the other end, but she wasn't sure. "No problem. I heard what happened. Congratulations on your new job."

"Thanks!" She said, "It's so exciting. Did you know I'm going to be on the news tomorrow night?"

"Yeah, that's pretty cool."

Kat leaned back on her bed, content. She saw the echo of her goofy grin in the mirror where the moonlight hit it. Then, the mirror reflected confusion.

"Wait a minute. How did you hear about all of this?"

"Well," Duncan hesitated before speaking nonchalantly. "I got worried about you when you didn't call. I called your phone and no one answered. I called your house and no one answered. I got concerned maybe you hadn't charged your battery or something on your phone since you were so excited about preparing for the shoot, so I drove by the school. I mean, a pretty girl like you shouldn't be left in a scary place like that all alone."

Kat imagined the warmth of his breath as he spoke.

"So what happened when you didn't find me?"

"I talked to someone who told me what had happened. I was happy for you."

Kat's eyes narrowed. "Who did you talk to?"

His voice sounded calm. "Bunny. The other girls all left while she was talking to me. I don't know if they even knew she was there. I had just missed you, and they must have thought she went with you guys." That explained the girls' phone call. "Anyway, like I said, I couldn't leave a girl in such a scary place as school, so I took her home and she told me all about your new job and how great you'd done with the team."

Pretty girl. He'd said that she was a pretty girl in a scary place. "So, how did you find out about the interview? That didn't happen until later tonight."

"Yeah, well. . ." he actually stammered. He never stammered. Duncan always knew exactly what he was doing. He planned almost as well as Kat. "We were hungry so we stopped by Sonic and grabbed something to eat. We just kept talking and... you know, she's funny."

"Yeah. She's a laugh a minute."

"Well *she* really likes *you*. She talked a lot about you and asked questions about us and stuff. She's nice."

"I bet she was," said Kat.

"What's that supposed to mean?"

"You never answered my question."

Again, he sounded uneasy. "What?"

"How did you know about my interview if you got a quick bite to eat and then took her home?"

"Well, we talked longer than we thought."

Kat swallowed hard and her ear hurt from her pressing the phone so hard against it. Her mouth felt dry. "How long?"

"When I dropped her off, her mom was home. I met her mom and she told me all about your great work. I'm really proud of you."

"How did you meet her mom if you just 'dropped her off'?" Kat was beginning to feel the first signs of panic. Kat knew she was prettier than Bunny, but she had made her look impeccable for the photo shoot. She'd used a lot of the magic dust and the girl had looked downright glamorous. *Maxim* would have asked her to pose for the magazine cover if they'd seen her.

Duncan's voice was exasperated. "I walked her to the door. Isn't that what a nice guy does?"

"On a date!"

"Kat, you're tired. I'm tired." He drew in a long breath. "You know you're my girl. I'm not starting a collection. Let's talk about this tomorrow."

"Whatever."

She hung up the phone and glared at her reflection. At that moment, she didn't care if she was creating wrinkles.

CHAPTER 34

The smell of popcorn filled the air as Duncan and Kat sat on the loveseat in her living room. She'd snubbed him sufficiently before answering his fifth call that day. She finally relented, allowing him to come to her house and watch her on TV.

"'Teen Focus' is on!" yelled Kat as the electric guitar version of the television station's theme music raged from the speakers.

Her parents hurried into the room, setting a bowl of popcorn on the coffee table in front of Duncan. They managed to sit down and catch their breath before the interview began.

"This is Eve Herrald with this week's 'Teen Focus.' We have with us tonight an enchanting young lady who is changing the face of Forrester. Kat Bonner. Good evening, Kat."

Kat smiled into the camera, drawing the attention of viewers everywhere.

Mrs. Herrald talked about how Kat had started her own business of beauty consulting. She managed to omit that her first day of work had been the day before.

"What beauty products do you use that work so well?" Herrald inquired.

Kat possessed the appearance some teenage girls get when they look innocent and vixen-ish at the same time. Remote controls across the metro ceased their clicking when the camera focused on her and the result of her handiwork, Eve Herrald. "A little bit of everything, Mrs. Herrald. But there's a final touch I kind of put together myself."

Herrald leaned forward. She could market this. Viewers listened carefully, too. This interview was better than the fashion magazines touting the top ten (or twenty or one hundred) secrets of beautiful women. "What's in it?"

The camera focused on Kat's flawless complexion as Kat raised her perfectly arched eyebrow. "Magic."

Duncan was not the only male viewer who felt uneasy when her interview was over, but he was uncomfortable because he suspected... the truth. As her parents gushed and the news changed to something else, he contemplated confronting her until she faced him and said, "So, what did you think?"

He was still curious, but after looking at her wasn't so sure. How could someone who looked so perfect be evil? All he could muster in reply was "Donald Trump, look out. A new mogul's in town."

"I doubt he'll be too concerned about a beauty mogul," Kat said.

"I don't know," her father contributed between handfuls of popcorn. "He does have a vested interest in all those pageants. Miss Teen, Miss America, Miss—"

A ringing telephone interrupted him. Kat's mom scurried to get it. A few moments later, she re-entered the room with a baffled expression. "The phone was for you, Kat."

Kat sat up. "Who is it?"

"I told him you'd call back. First, we need to talk."

Kat's body grew hot. Her head tingled and she felt a little dizzy. She remembered feeling this way each time her parents called, "Kat! Get in here! We need to talk." The conversations ended with "We're very disappointed in you."

She'd been caught. Somehow someone had figured out that she was kidnapping Little People, or were they chameleons? Unconsciously she reached for Duncan's hand. He held it with the twisted logic of one who holds someone who is about to be sentenced for a crime he knew she committed but still hoped she hadn't.

"The caller wanted to convey some very interesting news and do something more... unusual," her mom said slowly. To Kat, her mother seemed to be soaking in the knowledge her daughter, who had been given every opportunity for success, had chosen the path that went straight to the deepest domains of hell. The woman's eyes even filled with tears.

Feelings of... guilt?... once again permeated Kat. She hadn't meant to do anything wrong. She could still return the creatures before the police arrived. Would her parents have to move because of the embarrassment of having a daughter who was such a disappointment? Would she be allowed to wear her own underwear in jail?

Her mom spoke again. "Kat." Kat watched her mom look proudly at her father. "Kat, that was a reporter from *Newsweek*. He wants to interview you. Tonight."

Kat and Duncan each let out a huge breath and then looked at each other and started laughing. "Why?" asked Kat.

"He saw the interview—including the players' before and after photos." She peered over her eyeglasses. "He's traveling through town for something else and is leaving tonight. The magazine is running a feature on beauty in America. He said you might not get in the magazine. It would be 'just under the wire' he said. But he likes the fact that while most teenagers are self-absorbed, you go about the business of helping others. So, do you want to do it? It's up to you, Sis."

Kat's dreams were coming true.

CHAPTER 35

Duncan's Mustang slid into Kat's driveway right after breakfast. They went to school together to get their schedules for the approaching school year. As they exited the building, journalism students, wearing shorts and matching t-shirts, distributed the year's first edition of *Knightly News*, the school newspaper, and tried to get kids to buy subscriptions. They were mostly successful with the freshmen since many of them were driven to school by their parents who wanted to "stay connected" with their "babies" during the teenage years.

"Here you go, Kat!" said one of the students as she thrust the newspaper at her. "You're on the front page!" A throng of students pushed the couple past the newspaper jockey.

Duncan, whose arm had been resting around Kat's shoulder, deftly slipped through the crowd to get one of his own. When he returned, he said, "Want an ice cream?"

How could she resist a guy offering her Rocky Road on a sugar cone?

His Mustang eased into a parking place on the town square, a large patch of grass in the center of Forrester hemmed in by a sidewalk. The grass should have been green, but the Oklahoma August heat had turned it a premature yellow. In the center of the square squatted an old building. At one point the structure had been an American Indian tribe's council house but now was the county courthouse. The square was the traditional business district of town, and shops lined the streets surrounding it. Stores selling furniture, antiques, formal wear, video games, and comic books nestled beside a soda shop, hotdog stand, and café. The square had been there since the town's inception. Kat's grandparents told stories of "the good old days" when everyone gathered on the square each Saturday to have a picnic. It was the one day that rural families traveled into town for supplies. Kat found that hard to imagine since she lived in what would have been considered "the country" and her family went "to town" every day to work or to grab a gallon of milk. Duncan opened the soda shop door for her. *Serving Forrester since 1955* was printed on a sign taped to the glass on opening day. A bell hanging from the hand rail of the door jingled as they entered. Lining the walls were black and white photographs documenting Forrester's history.

"Stool or booth?" asked Kat. Duncan looked at the chrome stools lining the bar and grabbed her hand. "Booth." Duncan pulled her next to him, and they propped their feet up on the opposite bench. "Now," he said as he popped open the newspaper. "What does the *Knightly News* say about Forrester's new basketball hero?" He lowered the paper and wiggled his eyebrows. "First, let's see what it says about our fair Kat."

Kat proffered a protest, but liked to hear nice things about herself. "We really don't have to."

Duncan pulled her close and kissed the top of her head. "I can't believe how modest you are." Then he read the article aloud as one hand rested on the back of her neck, his fingers lightly tugging her hair.

What high school student doesn't need fashion advice at some point in his or her four (hopefully not five) year stint at Forrester High? Now no student needs to worry about hiding that pepperoni-sized pimple.

Kat Bonner, sophomore, is fashionable and fabulous. Her generosity not only extends to the beauty she creates in her clients, but also she helped to launch the modeling careers of several of Forrester High's soccer team.

Local news anchor Eve Herrald had a few words to say about Bonner. 'She is mature and calculating in her attack on flaws. I feel better knowing she's fighting the battle for me. I'm guaranteed a beautiful, happy ending.

"Too bad Bunny and the others won't be here for the first part of school," said Kat not meaning it in the least but managing to sound sincere.

"I'm sure they won't mind," said Duncan. "After all they're doing photo shoots for those magazines—what are they called?"

"*Seventeen, YM, Teen Vogue.*"

"Hmmm. I'm sure it's torture for them not getting to go through the first week of school where all you do is try not to sleep as you re-read the dress code and rules in every class. It must be tough to be at a beach somewhere hanging around a lot of other hot models."

Kat cocked her head and her eyebrow shot up. So he thought they were all "hot"?

Duncan looked down at the paper to begin reading again.

Kat said, "They're shooting the Easter issue. They're in Australia where it's cold. They're wearing parkas."

"What was I thinking?" Duncan feigned frustration. "It must be horrible for them to be nice and cool while we're boiling in this heat. What's the temp today? 110? It does seem to be cooling down for the fall."

She slapped his knee.

"What? What'd I say?"

"You stopped reading." Looking at her watch she said, "I've

got to get going soon." She paused to savor the idea. "Interview with *Teen People.*"

Duncan read dutifully:

Featured in Newsweek *magazine as a teen entrepreneur, she claims she plans to stay grounded. Since that first of many national magazine articles and interviews was published, movie production companies, international modeling agencies and others have contacted her, but Bonner states, 'I just can't imagine being able to work my magic if I stay away from home too long. What I require to spread the beauty, I find right here in Forrester.*

Duncan lowered the paper, and his face was solemn. "I know the truth. Your confession was all I needed." Kat's throat suddenly hurt and her pulse surged through her chest and arms. He grinned. "You just don't want to be away from me."

Before Kat could answer, the waitress appeared at the table. Between chomps of her gum she asked, "What's your poison?"

CHAPTER 36

The People rode rattlesnakes and frogs. The invasion had begun. Naturals surrounded Kat's window. Weapons, capable of varying degrees of destruction, lay on the ground or waited, suspended in mid-air, for use.

Thorne hovered in front of the middle of the window and warned, "Use your Glamour sparingly because we want to leave no Naturals here tonight. Ours is a covert operation. No light has shone from the fairy hunter's window, so we must assume she is away and will not return during our rescue operation. In case she does, the element of surprise is always our greatest weapon."

Thorne turned to Blaezi standing at his side, and she jerked her head toward Laurel. She whispered, "He wants to do it. I can't talk him out of it."

Laurel spoke to the cluster of Naturals gathered to help. "Since I know the terrain of the hunter's realm, I'll lead you." The People glowed with enthusiasm in a silent cheer. Any human looking in the direction of Kat's window would think a great bunch of fireflies had descended around it. Laurel's tail was not full-grown, but he backed himself up to the window anyway. Dragging his tail across the glass surface, he created a glimmering bull's-eye. When the final circle was complete, he moved slowly away from the window. Thorne and Blaezi exchanged glances as Dogwood caught Laurel's weak body. The People on the front row heard Laurel whisper,

"Let's go get Rock."

Thorne's tiny trebuchets made of twigs and walnuts were the first act of battle. Naturals felt the rush of air as river rocks sailed by them before crashing into the bull's-eye on the window, but they never heard the crash. They only saw it. Laurel's tail had enough Glamour in it to silence the breaking glass. A few stones hit the window screen and punctured it, but the holes weren't big enough for the invading army. When the trebuchets ceased catapulting, Naturals, holding jagged flint rock, advanced on the enemy's position and cut the screen. They rolled the mesh back like a petal. Laurel moved slowly toward the opening and motioned everyone to follow him. They did. The room was dark, and the smell of stale Glamour hung in the air.

Just inside, Laurel collapsed on the window sill, too drained to fly. He pointed to the box on the vanity. "In there!"

A group advanced to the prison while others spread out around the room, ready to guard their escape. Although the room was dark, they identified each other by the glittery reflection of their tails in the moonlight. The group of Naturals moved toward the lid to lift it but was quickly repelled. Their wings dropped and their bodies hung limp in the air.

"What?" whispered Laurel. "What's wrong?"

"Iron!" Thorne called when he approached to inspect it. No wonder the Naturals had weakened in captivity; iron could be fatal. He called more People to the box lid and told them, "I know it weakens us, but we can do this. We *must* do this or our entire existence is at stake."

"Why must they do it?" Blaezi ordered them. "Save your strength. One of the animals who isn't weakened by iron will do it."

Thorne muttered, "You're pretty clever for a Faye" and disappeared out the window. A few moments later, four dark-mottled rattlesnakes, ridden by Naturals, wound their ways up the vanity toward the box. They attempted to nudge open the box, but instead knocked it off the table with their triangular-shaped heads. Unlike the window, they hadn't placed a silencing charm on the box so it clattered to the floor, spilling wounded Naturals everywhere.

Due to their absence of Glamour, the captives couldn't be seen in the moonlight. But their cheer was heard: a hollow, weak cry full of relief and fear.

As they'd practiced during drills, the Naturals placed the wounded on the rattlesnakes, which then slithered out the window. A couple of snakes remained as sentinels. The Naturals formed a line and passed off each tail-less, tortured prisoner one to the other out of the box, across the room, and through the window. Outside, the wounded were placed on the brown backs of large rattlesnakes. When given the go ahead, the snakes glided through the weeds toward the woods where Raine waited to heal the injured.

The skinny, wide-eyed Naturals seemed to keep coming from the box. They must have been piled tightly with little room to breathe. The stronger ones helped to get the weaker ones out first. Finally, Thorne and Blaezi saw a thinner version of Rock. He was the last one in the box. Thorne rushed to him and picked him up. Blaezi couldn't help but think that the Natural wouldn't be in this position if he hadn't wished her ill, but she also felt almost a twinge of compassion for anything treated as the captives had been.

She didn't have long to ponder empathy because the overhead light switched on. Kat appeared in the doorway wearing a pink towel on her head and a matching towel around her body. "What's going on in here?" she mumbled before shrieking, "OUCH!" when she stepped on one of the river rocks. She looked up and saw the window that had been broken and cut. Gripping her towel tighter, she looked around the room for an intruder, and her eyes fell on the vanity. Instead of the box full of Naturals, she was greeted by a rattle from a snake, coiled and ready to strike. She stumbled toward her bed, but her ankles and bare legs met sharp pains. Naturals had hidden themselves among her pillows and bed ruffles and were now barraging her with cocklebur maces. She rushed to the other side of the room, almost stepping on another snake on his way out the window.

"Quick!" called Thorne, "Get him on the rattler and get him out of here!" Laurel crawled on the snake as Thorne and Blaezi helped load Rock onto it. Thorne slapped its side and it slithered away. The Naturals cleared the room in twenty seconds, but Thorne wanted to make sure everyone was gone. He turned to Blaezi. "Ask her if she has more."

She tugged him toward the window. "Why? It's not like we can save them tonight. We'll have to come back."

"Blaezi. You don't have any more nights left. If you want to go home, you'll have to finish this tonight. Look at the moon!"

Kat finished picking the cockleburs from her skin. Droplets of blood were on her legs, and her anger was full throttle. She grabbed a magazine from her bed and, clutching it tightly, swatted at them. Thorne and Blaezi leapt in separate directions.

Anger surged Blaezi's courage. "Human, do you have any other of our People or did we take them all from you?"

No answer from Kat except a quick swat with her *Teen People*. Blaezi rolled to avoid the magazine. Her hair whooshed with the force of the blow, and the tips of her right wings suffered paper cuts.

Thorne called to her, "You go to the window since you're closer, I'll go the way she came in and meet you outside." Blaezi hesitated, and Thorne yelled, "Go!"

So she went. Kat pursued her until Thorne flew straight toward Kat's face and tweaked her nose. Enraged, Kat lifted the magazine and swatted herself in the face. Thorne laughed so hard he barely made it out of her bedroom door before she slammed it. He wasn't sure of the path to get out, but his sense of direction was good. He located the front door.

Thorne used his Glamour to open it but stopped when he saw the exterior door. It was one of those safety doors created from iron bars. Thorne had never before encountered iron in such a large quantity. Weakness took his body, and Kat easily scooped him up in one hand.

CHAPTER 37

Blaezi exited the bedroom window and ordered the troupe to meet at the front porch. As Kat stepped outside, hands clasped in triumph, she nearly stepped on a multitude of eerily silent frogs, ridden by determined Naturals. She took a step back, and a rattle caused every muscle in her body to tense. Dogwood's voice carried on the air. "Now!" Sharpened sweet gum balls assailed her. In an attempt to avoid the snakes and the frogs as well as dodge the bombardment of sharp spikes pelting her exposed body, she took a sideways step and slipped on the brown sweet gum balls clustered like marbles on the porch.

The impact with the concrete slab brought tears to her eyes, but Kat held her hands high. "Call them off!" She gave her hands a shake and the People heard Thorne's muffled cry. Kat couldn't understand what he said, but Blaezi did. She flew above the cavalry and demanded, "Human, return the captive."

"And why should I?" smirked Kat, looking threatening even though the towel on her head had slipped a little. She moved to straighten it, and the snakes rattled their tails. "Little Person," she spoke between clinched teeth, "you better call off those snakes and frogs or I won't discuss anything with you." She squinted her eyes. "Aren't you the one who wanted to negotiate?" She thrust a haughty chin into the air. "Well, *this* is no way to negotiate."

Blaezi considered the strange natures of humans. "Fine," she said and instructed the others to retreat. They moved back, and as soon as they did Kat leapt to her feet, opened the front door, and slipped behind the safety of the iron bars. Blaezi was glad Rock wasn't there to see her mistake. Though she'd rescued him, he would never let her live down this crucial error. She could feel the other Naturals' eyes on her as well as a sliver of the moon's rays.

Blaezi pretended Kat's retreat had gone according to plan. "Feel better now? Let's get down to business." Blaezi approached as closely as she dared and said, "In exchange for your captive and food, we will give you—"

"Food?" Kat laughed so hard she almost snorted. "Who said anything about food?"

"I did." Blaezi's voice didn't quiver, but her wings did. Her time was almost gone. The night was late. "As I was saying, in exchange for your captive and food, we will give you portions of Glamour."

Kat's features softened and she spoke in a hushed tone. "Glamour? What's 'Glamour'?"

Blaezi put her hands on her hips. "You know very well what Glamour is and does. It's why you keep stealing our tails!"

A smile flickered on Kat's lips. "And I must say you have the most beautiful one I've seen yet." She raised her eyebrows. "How much is a portion of Glamour?"

"Enough."

Kat sighed. "I don't know. I don't see why I should trust you. I'm getting pretty famous and can't afford to lose this little bit of magic right now." She gave her hands, and Thorne, a shake. "I think I'll keep him around a while. Besides, I can always get a new one if anything happens to him." She looked at the congregation. "I can see there are lots more." She stepped back to close the door. "Ta-ta! You can find your own twigs and berries to eat." The door slammed an end to the negotiations.

Blaezi flinched as Dogwood's hand squeezed her. "Blaezi, there's nothing we can do right now. Come back to camp, and we'll plan our next attack. Maybe Raine has managed to get some of the newly released Naturals able to talk. They might give us advice on rescuing Thorne."

Blaezi's strength was zapped. She looked up at the moon. "I guess you're right. We must do all we can."

"We'll get him back, Blaezi. Don't worry." He maneuvered her to follow the rest of the retreating Naturals. "It's nice of you to help us so much when you don't have to."

All of the pain in Blaezi's muscles and heart went to her throat. She swallowed. "Dogwood, you're wrong. I do have to help you. There's something I've got to tell you. Tell all of you."

He gripped her shoulder more tightly and said, "No, you don't. We know enough, Blaezi. We know more than you think we do." He hugged her then. A quick hug. He said, "Let's go home."

But Blaezi couldn't go home. She jerked away from Dogwood and flew back toward the house. "You go on! Learn what you can! I'll catch up!" She was so determined and quick that Dogwood let her go.

Before she realized what she'd done, Blaezi had flown through the broken window, through the torn screen, and was sitting on Kat's window sill. The human puttered around her bedroom. Although it was late evening, she appeared to be getting ready to go out. Blaezi had no way of knowing that bedtime was when Kat experimented with new "looks." Thorne was nowhere to be seen, but the box was closed and resting again on the vanity.

Blaezi clinched her fists. How could she just exist as if she had done nothing wrong? Her voice spoke as loud as three humans. "If you're so good at capturing us, why haven't you caught me yet?"

Kat swiveled quickly, curling iron in hand.

"You've seen me several times. You've never caught me." Blaezi stood and leaned against the sill as she sighed, "I don't think you can." She pranced along the window sill, strutting her glorious tail. A small ray of moonlight spilled onto Blaezi, and Kat watched the orange, red, and yellow strands of Blaezi's tail glisten. With a swish of her tail, Blaezi said, "Just imagine all that you could do with this tail."

Kat stared in awe. The tail was nothing short of... glamorous.

Blaezi continued to taunt her without straying too far from the safety of an exit. "You mentioned being able to catch us when you want, but I don't think you can. We've not had anyone missing since you caught Rock. You know, the ugly, square guy with the mangy tail?" She shrugged. "Not that I can blame you." Blaezi leaned forward, feigning interest. "Was it a personal choice? Believe me, if I'd captured him, I'd think twice before doing it again, too."

Kat laughed and held out the curling iron as if it were a teacher's pointer stick. "Believe me, I've caught others."

Blaezi forced a laugh. "Yeah, right. I guess next thing you'll say is you've got them hidden somewhere else in the room?"

Kat placed the curling iron neatly on the vanity and strolled to a corner of the room where a yellow bird cage dangled. She swiftly removed a pink cover, revealing three prisoners: Thorne, Diana, and Dion. She smiled at Blaezi. "I cover these because they talk too much—like you." She batted her eyes.

Blaezi stopped strutting. Diana and Dion's frail bodies resembled those they had hundreds of summers ago when they were children and played in the woods. Blaezi murmured, "You tried to help me after all."

Dion managed to say, "We... tried."

Diana added, "We knew your time was ending..." She took a ragged breath. ". . . and we missed you."

Thorne finished for them. He was weak, but he was angry enough to find strength. "They came to help you with your tasks so you could go home." He gave her a nod. "Good friends."

What could Blaezi do? The fairy hunter had her oldest and dearest friends, and she had her newest one, too. Blaezi had to offer a sacrifice. Her for them.

"Are you still open to negotiations?" asked Blaezi.

Kat folded the bird cage cover, squaring each corner, and set it on a chair. She acted bored. "Sure, why not?"

"In exchange for the prisoners and food, I'll... I'll..." she swallowed. Her tail tingled with her wings and she felt strong. "I'll give you my tail."

Kat frowned briefly. "Why would I want to do something like that? You offered me Glamour before. I don't need your tail." She walked over to the birdcage and gave it a jiggle. The captives sprawled to the bottom of the cage. She turned to Blaezi as if posing and smiled. "I've got three tails right here. That's all I need. I could breed them and get all I want. Your single, measly little tail won't possibly be enough for my work."

Blaezi flew dangerously close to Kat before realizing she'd left the safety of the window. "First of all, you don't know anything! You won't be able to breed them—not the way you treat us. Second of all, my tail is different. Haven't you noticed that? It's not your ordinary *fairy* tail—it's mine."

Kat swiped at her with her hand, but Blaezi's speed was faster than Kat expected. Blaezi was on the window sill again before Kat realized she hadn't caught her.

"They grow back, ya know," cooed Blaezi. "Not the way you hold us. But in nature, they grow back." Blaezi's voice took on a magical, alluring quality. "Mine is special. Mine grows back many moons faster than the others."

She glanced up at the moon and panic filled her. Not only would she be banished, but also she would be to blame for endangering two Fayes and a Natural. No one, not even Dogwood or Laurel, would forgive her. And she couldn't blame them.

She gave it one last try. "Release them. I'll leave you my tail as soon as food is deposited at the tree where you met me. It's the right thing to do. It's a good agreement."

"Dream on," hissed Kat.

"I'd prefer less primitive methods, but...." Blaezi sent forth a yellow stream of Glamour, and the vanity mirror burst. Blaezi was outside the window when she said, "Have it your way, then. Here's your warning: until you take my offer, all magic will go bad."

CHAPTER 38

A breeze blew through the holes in the window and whipped the curtains into a frenzy. Kat had not re-covered the birdcage, so Diana, Dion, and Thorne soaked up the moon's rays and gained some much needed strength. Kat's cell phone rang and awakened her from a fitful sleep.

"Ka-a-a-at!" shrieked a tiny voice on the other end.

"Who's this?" Sleep was thick in Kat's voice.

The distant voice verged on hysteria. The caller cried so much that Kat instinctively wiped her ear as if some of the girl's tears had spilled through the phone. Kat repeated, annoyed, "Who is this? And speak up. I can't hear you very well."

More sobbing erupted. "Kat, it's Bunny. You've..." *gasp* "...got..." *gasp* "... to do something!"

Kat sat up in bed and looked at her clock: 3 AM. "What's wrong with you?" Bunny sobbed harder, so Kat softened her voice. "Aren't you at a photo shoot?"

"Yeeeeeees!"

"Calm down," cooed Kat. "Tell me what's wrong." She gulped as she eyed the birdcage. "I'm... sure we can fix it."

"I can't shave my legs!" yelled Bunny. "I've tried and tried, but I can't shave them."

Blaezi let out a deep breath and rolled her eyes. "Get them waxed, then." *This* is what she was waking her up about at 3 in the morning?

"Kat," replied a hostile Bunny, "you're missing the point. I *have* had them waxed. I *have* shaved them. They just won't *stay* that way."

Kat twirled a strand of hair around her finger and asked, "Does it really matter? Aren't you in Australia doing a winter spread? Don't they have you wearing fur coats or something?"

"Nooooo!" wailed Bunny. "And you know I'd only wear faux. I went to Paris instead and we're. . . we're. . . we're wearing swimsuits." She sobbed again into the phone. "Tell me what to do."

"Easy," Kat said. "Add some of the sparkle I gave you and it should be fine."

"That's just it, Kat!" She sniffled, indicating an end to the crying fit. "I used all of it already. I think that's the problem. What happens if I use too much?" The prisoners in the birdcage giggled. Dion called, "Has Blaezi's curse started already?"

"Ooohh, there'll be more," whispered Diana. "I've never heard the Faye so mad. Have you, Dion?"

"Never."

The female chattered something to the newly captured fairy and then they all collapsed in giggles under the moonlight.

Kat turned away from the taunting and said, "Don't talk crazy, Bunny. You can't use too much of my product. It's good for you. It's all natural and even healthy. There's nothing it can do to hurt you or make anyone look less than glamorous."

"But—"

Kat's voice became tense. "No 'buts'. You must have used something else. You had your legs waxed. That might be it."

"I've done that before Kat."

"In Paris?"

"Well... no."

"There you go." Kat was quite pleased at how easy manipulating clients was turning out to be. "Have you done anything else potentially damaging?"

"I used a self-tanner."

"Bunny!" screeched Kat, pretending to be horrified. "I can't believe you. With my product, you should never have to use anything else." She turned back to look at the prisoners to make sure they heard her and said, "Clearly, you have no one to blame for this fiasco but yourself. Now, I've got to get my beauty sleep. Good night."

She hit the "end" button and switched off the phone as quickly as possible. After chunking the phone at the birdcage and hitting it, she drifted off to sleep, smiling at the clanging noise the collision created as well as the screams of the creatures.

CHAPTER 39

Between the nagging of the creatures in the birdcage and the August heat coming through the window, Kat got little "beauty sleep." Instead, she awoke, sweaty and irritable, to another phone call. When she removed the damp pillow she had wrapped around her head in an attempt to block out the noise, she felt the puffiness weighing beneath her eyes. She squinted at the clock again. 6:36. Ugh. Her cell phone would not stop ringing. Hadn't she turned it off? She really hated people who called, left a message, called, left a message, etc. Why were they so needy? And what normal person called this early?

Grudgingly she padded over to where the phone lay after ricocheting off the birdcage. When she bent over to pick it up, one of the creatures stuck out his tongue. "Thbbbt!"

Kat stood up straight and glared at them. "Are you…? How? Are you turning on my phone?"

"Ah, ah, ah. You better be nice to us," the female waggled her finger at her. "We're the ones who can help you out of this mess."

"What mess?" spat Kat as she silenced the ring on her phone again. "I'm in no mess. And if I were, I wouldn't need a little chameleon or whatever-you-are to get me out of it."

Dion laughed at her. "Miss, we're not chameleons. As we tried to tell you a few evenings ago when you captured us, Diana and I are Fayes." He jerked his head toward Thorne. "He's a Natural."

Dion, imperious, then looked down his tiny nose at Kat before he crossed his arms and grinned. "And you, my dear, are in big, big trouble."

Kat grabbed the cover and yanked it over the cage to silence them. She didn't even pause when she heard their screams of terror.

Disgusted, she flipped open her phone to check her messages, but she had apparently answered another incoming call instead because a woman's voice was saying, "Hello? Kat, is that you? Hello!"

"Yeah?" grumbled Kat, who felt even grumpier when she caught a whiff of her armpit.

"Kat, this is Eve Herrald."

Kat turned to sugar. "Why, hello, Mrs. Herrald. It's awfully early, don't you think? Not that it matters," Kat lied. "It's always a delight to hear from you. Thanks for checking in on me while my parents are out of town for a few days. Don't worry. I'll call if I need anything, but I doubt I'll bother you."

"Cut the crap, Kat. What have you put in your makeup? Bunny is on a plane right now to come home. Several of her contracts cancelled on her due to her, um, hairy situation. I've already contacted my lawyer."

Kat began to panic but her voice remained steady. "Now, Mrs. Herrald, I think it is a very good idea to get someone to help you. A contract is a contract, after all."

"The lawyer isn't for the contracts, you prissy little idgit, he's to sue you!"

Kat heard the muffled, yet pained giggles of the creatures beneath the cover.

"Mrs. Herrald!" Kat nervously twirled her hair around her finger. "I'm astonished you would consider such a thing! Why would you go and sue someone like me?"

"You know why! You've ruined my daughter's career. And mine!"

Kat felt as if someone's hands had encircled her throat and squeezed. "How so?" she managed to get out.

"I have cold sores."

Tension eased a bit around her throat as she considered this ailment. "Tell me, Mrs. Herrald, how that is my fault. Just like in Bunny's situation, there is nothing I've done to cause it. On the other hand," she twisted her hair ferociously, "can't stress bring on cold sores? I mean, your teenage daughter is flying all over the world wearing very few clothes and getting her picture taken by a lot of strange men that you don't even know."

As if Mrs. Herrald hadn't been threatening enough, her voice turned to acid. "Just what are you implying, Kat Bonner? My Bunny is a good girl and you have no right to suggest otherwise. I trust her completely."

Kat assumed she had pushed too far. "Oh, of course, Mrs. Herrald. As you know, Bunny is a dear, dear friend of mine. You have every reason to trust her. I just figured you must miss her and worry about what other people might be up to, that's all." She needed to change the subject. Parents can be so touchy about their children. "Also, your career has taken a few positive turns as well. Although it's good, it's bound to be stressful."

"Yes, well..." Mrs. Herrald's voice had lost the ice.

"Don't worry, Mrs. Herrald. I assure you there is nothing in my makeup or treatments to cause such outlandish things to happen."

Eve Herrald melted. "Oh, Kat, I'm so sorry. I know you're right. Do you think you could come over and do my makeup for—"

"Oops. Sorry to interrupt you, but I've got to go. I have a very important call coming in." Kat hung up on her and collapsed on the floor. As soon as she hit the ground her phone rang again. Chaos continued for several hours until she had returned at least sixty-three messages and avoided at least fifty-two lawsuits.

Finally, Kat was able to put the phone on its charger and sink into her carpet. The sun was high and hot, and she smelled worse than any dirty cat box. Her stomach grumbled, so she decided to grab a bagel before taking a shower.

Kat retrieved her warm bagel from the microwave and screamed. The reflection screaming back at her was hideous. She rushed to her room to get a clearer picture in her cracked vanity mirror. She only screamed louder.

On her usually petite nose was the largest wart she had ever seen. The puffy bags beneath her eyes were a dark black and a freckle she had on her right cheek cultivated a very long, very dark hair. She scrambled for her tweezers and quickly plucked the offending hair. Just as quickly, it sprouted back darker and longer. Her eyes grew wide with fear, and she placed her hands over her ears to block out the horrible screaming—hers.

CHAPTER 40

The prisoners trembled as Kat pressed her warty nose through the iron bars of the cage and spat at them. "Fix it! Fix all of it!" Furious, she whacked the cage with the cover she held in her hand. The cage reacted obligingly to the action and swung, knocking her in the face as it went. "Owwwwggh!" She jerked her head back, dropped the cover, and held her injured nose. For the first time, the trio saw tears form in her eyes.

Thorne said, "Maybe she's more natural than we thought."

"No," said Diana. "She's crying because she hurt herself."

Kat sprang forward again, "What? What are you saying? I can't understand you. Speak English or... or..." she collapsed at the foot of the birdcage and real tears formed, "or I don't know what I'll do."

"Those," said Diana cheerfully, "are not tears from physical pain. Those tears are from heart pain."

Dion studied her. "Do you really think she regrets what she's done?"

"No," said Thorne. "She just regrets getting caught and looking ugly." He shivered. "Really ugly."

Between sobs resembling those of Bunny's, Kat said, "Stop talking about me. Speak English!" Her hands, clenched in fists, beat the air.

Dion and Diana laughed. They translated to Thorne, and they

all collapsed in fits of laughter. Even laughing took extra energy when behind iron bars.

Dion spoke to Kat first. "Human, release us and do as Blaezi commanded, and all will be well. Curses of this magnitude are rarely made anymore."

Curled up in the fetal position on the floor, Kat sniffled and wiped her runny nose with the knee of her pink silk pajama pants. One thumb secured like a lollipop in her mouth. Just when she seemed about to gain control of her emotions, the tears flowed again. She slobbered, "Who's Blaezi?"

Although Thorne didn't speak English, he recognized Blaezi's name and guessed what she was asking. "Tell her she's the Faye with the most beautiful tail."

Dion took a step back from Thorne, surprised by the description of his friend. Diana pinched his wing and Dion translated.

Kat nodded and spoke around her thumb. "How do I know you won't leave me this way if I let you go?!"

Diana spoke next, her voice smooth. "We are not the sort of People to resort to tricks with humans unless you push us too far. You pushed Blaezi too far." Dion, trying to hold back a chuckle, ended up making an odd sound instead, followed by snorting laughter. Diana said, "If you release us and follow her orders, she'll lift her curse. It's as easy as flying." Dion nudged her. She frowned. "Or... sucking your thumb?"

Kat sat upright, still clutching her knees, and rocked back and forth. She removed her thumb and wiped it on her pajama pants. Her hands slowly moved to her hair and smoothed it out. The fact that it sprang back to disarray seemed not to faze her. Kat's eyes settled on the creatures with a cold stare and her lips twitched into a small, tight, calculated smile. "Did you say, 'sort of *people*'?"

The three creatures exchanged concerned glances. Had this

human lost her mind? Was she hard of hearing? Dion yelled, "Yes!"

Kat stood and walked gracefully to the cage, the strange smile still on her lips. "Let me get this straight. You call yourselves, Fayes, Naturals, and People?"

Diana translated to Thorne. They all turned to Kat and nodded in proud agreement.

Kat said, "Do you consider yourself *little* People?"

Diana looked at her small body, and then Kat's before saying, "What do you think?"

Kat turned abruptly on her heels, picked up her bagel that had landed on the floor and tossed it in the trashcan.

"Hey!" cried Dion. "We would eat that. You haven't fed us today, you know."

"Oh!" Kat placed her delicate hands, also covered in warts, to her mouth and said, "Pardon *moi*." She reached into the wastebasket, gingerly pulled out the bagel, and pushed it through the bars of the bird cage.

"You could let us out at least to eat," said Dion. "It's not like we're strong enough to leave."

Diana jumped in, "—unless you decide to let us go."

Kat almost cackled. "Oh, my little People, I'm not going to let you go! Now that I know what you are, I just need to know what to do about you." And again, she turned on her heels and walked away from the birdcage. Unshowered and unmadeup, she sat in front of her computer and researched.

***

Journal Entry

*****Notes on Little People and fairies*****

appearance: diminutive to over six feet tall, may have wings or appear as humans

AKA in Europe: fay, faie, fey, leprechaun, pixie, elf, gnome, brownie, etc.

AKA by Cherokee: little people (other tribes have them, too)
Dates to remember:
March 21: dangerous for swimming—water fairies like to pull humans in
    June 21: Midsummer Eve—can see fairies dancing
    August 7: hills and dwellings revealed to any human eye
    September 29: doors open to mortal and fairy realms
    November 8: hills and dwellings revealed to any human eye

    Other ways to see fairies:
    Place wildflowers under pillow and dream of them
    At dusk or evening
    Through water-bored stone found in tumbling brook
    Note to self: use one collected from first date with Duncan
    Potion of thyme
    Drops of calendula juice on eyelids

    Keep fairies away:
    Iron, bonfires, St. John's Wort, crosses on baked goods

    Dangers: They are known for causing disfigurement, kidnapping, and destruction when wronged. !!!
    *Their magical fairy dust is called Glamour.
    *No notes on Naturals
    *Most information on Little People concerns dwarfs
    Note to self: ask Duncan more about LP

Phone calls interrupted Kat as she attempted to research her creatures on the internet. During an interlude, Kat leaned back in her desk chair and reviewed her notes. She was tired of arguing.

Tired of being blamed for ugliness. And most of all, she was tired of *being* ugly. She frowned as she chewed the end of the pencil. She barely concerned herself with the wrinkles her frown was causing and the damage the pencil was doing to her teeth. If she couldn't get out of this fairy curse, she was doomed to be ugly forever. Furthermore, all of the people she had helped to make beautiful would be terminally ugly and hate her for it. She had postponed them for a day, but if they spoke to each other or word got out, no one would believe it wasn't her fault.

"Have you decided you're wrong yet?" asked Dion.

Kat replied by throwing her pencil at the cage. Thorne caught it and held it like a spear.

She perused an article from npr.org. Apparently, thousands of years ago a species of human about 3 feet tall lived on an island in Indonesia. Scientists speculated whether they evolved that way due to resources and predators or they were a separate species altogether. Some scientists doubted their existence and thought the remains were from a human who suffered from a disease; however, lore from neighboring islanders survived and was rife with tales of little people. Kat furrowed her brow in concentration.

Diana said, "If you'd ask us, we'd help you."

Kat shifted her eyes from the computer. "Okay. Have you always been this size?"

They translated to Thorne, and they chattered. Dion answered, "We have always been this size, but lore tells us at one time our people were as large as yours."

"How did you end up this way?"

"When we were larger, we were in danger. We grew smaller to protect ourselves," said Dion.

"A lot of good that's done us," muttered Diana.

Kat asked, "So, you're smaller to avoid predators?"

Dion translated to Thorne who glared at Kat. "Yes," he answered. "And because our forest is smaller."

Kat bit her lip. "Have you always had tails?"

Dion and Diana sighed before translating to Thorne who sighed, too.

"I'm tired of discussing this," Diana said. "Just do as Blaezi instructs and you will have no troubles."

Kat looked out her broken window toward the silhouette of forest. She jumped up and ran to her closet. She pulled off her pajamas to put on shorts and a t-shirt, but she noticed her legs had grown to resemble a chimp's overnight. She tore off the shorts and replaced them with jeans. She looked down at her feet and realized in horror that she was in desperate need of a pedicure even though she'd had one the day before. No time. She put on socks and sneakers, then grabbed her satchel and thrust her journal inside.

Next she unzipped a side pocket, opened the bird cage, and reached in for the prisoners. Her hand met a jabbing pencil-spear instead of the fluttery sensation of little bodies. She jerked her hand back and slammed the cage door.

"What did you do that for?" shrieked Kat as she vigorously shook her hand to free it of pain. "I'm taking you to the forest to let you go and you stab me!"

"Well, you should have said so in the first place," replied Diana.

"Just open the cage door and we'll follow," said Dion. "We might be a little slow, but we'll follow you."

"Nice try, but no," said Kat. "I'm not letting you out of my sight." She gave the birdcage stand a swift kick and Thorne dropped the pencil between the bars forming the grill of the floor. Kat retrieved it and dropped it in her bag with the journal. "Ooooh. Poor little guy. Did you drop your itty bitty torture device? Too bad!" Once again, she opened the cage door. This time, she wasn't stabbed and she grabbed all of them on the first try. She stuffed the captives into her satchel and zipped up the pocket.

Tiny imprints of feet and fists could be seen attempting to puncture the walls of the purse. "Settle down!" she said and gave the bag a severe jerk. Their movement became calmer, but the bag still writhed as if full of snakes.

CHAPTER 41

By the time Kat reached the area where she had seen Blaezi and first shared a picnic with Duncan, the stars were out and the sun almost gone. Her research indicated she could best see fairies at dusk or evening. She wiggled her satchel. "Hey, is this dusk yet?"

The bag responded with murmurs resembling cursing, but she couldn't discern the words. She shrugged her shoulders, jostling the contents of the bag. "Oh well. If you don't speak up, I can't hear you. You can stop trying to get me to let you out."

She heard a rustle and looked in the limbs above her. Her pulse quickened so much she could have sworn someone had IVed twenty sodas into her body. A black snake, almost six feet long from flickering tongue to vibrating tail flopped off the tree and landed at her feet. Actually, it partially landed *on* her feet, and the pain of her toes was crushing, yet she dared not breathe—much less scream. The snake must have sensed her fear because it turned, and Kat saw its eyes glint in the moonlight. Just as quickly as it had fallen and turned its head, it slithered in the direction of the river. On the back of the snake rode two Naturals. One faced front and directed the snake. The other held the rear and kept a tiny bow with arrow aimed at Kat. But it didn't release it.

"Hey!" Kat called. She dropped a plastic Wal-Mart sack filled with food she'd brought in case she needed to wait for them through dinner. She swung her arms wildly. "Hey! I want to talk to you!"

But the Naturals and snake were gone.

Surveying the area for fairies, she reached in the satchel and removed her journal. Her fingers flipped it open. A penlight dangled from her belt loop, which Kat unhooked and flashed over the journal to review. As she stuffed the book back in the bag, she decided she may have already missed dusk. She searched with her fingers for the stone she'd picked up with Duncan and remembered that in her rush she hadn't packed it. She made her way to the river to pick up a stone. She guessed she'd use it like a periscope into another world.

Kat took a deep breath and, cupping her hands to her mouth, yelled, "I'm ready to make a deal!"

The woods were uncharacteristically still. It seemed even the woodland creatures had been told to pretend they weren't at home. A breeze caught Kat's mangled hair and she brushed it from her eyes before collecting the sack and walking toward the river. She needed a water-bored stone.

The short distance to the water was difficult. Unseen twigs and roots seemed to leap from the ground and trip her. Time and again, Kat received an opportunity to taste dirt. After each of her falls, she heard far off laughter. At first she thought she imagined it, but after the seventh or eighth time, she was certain the laughter was real when the satchel twitched and she heard the muffled laughter of the captives within.

"I can hear you!" she spat. "You're lucky I don't land on any of you—especially the ones with me. You're not being very nice!" She didn't know if she were yelling at the fairies in the woods or at the ones in her satchel. It didn't matter. Her yells were once again answered by the silence of the moonbeams. However, she didn't fall anymore.

She felt she'd earned a medal once she reached the shoreline. She collapsed on her hands and knees and searched the stones for ones with holes. As she moved closer and closer to the water's edge, she remembered the day Bunny and Duncan had talked about the Little People and how they liked to pull humans into water. Immediately, she scrambled backward like a crawdad and continued her search.

The first pebble didn't hit her. The sound of clacking rock on rock caught her attention. So did the distant giggling. The next one was closer. Finally, when her fingers caressed a stone with a hole in it, a pebble pelted her on the hand holding it and the water-bored stone clattered back into the plethora of others looking just like it—except for the hole. Instead of giggles that time, she heard cheers.

She turned her face in the direction of the noise and called, "I'm not leaving until you swap with me! I want to make a deal. I... I *need* to make a deal." The only response was that she felt her eyebrows grow together.

She reached up to brush a long brow hair from her eyes so she could see. Tears of anger, then frustration, and finally desperation ran down her cheeks. "Fine!" She stood up, grabbed the food sack, and stomped in the direction of the tree. "I've not needed help in catching you before; I shouldn't need help seeing you now. Geez. All I want to do is 'negotiate.'" She paused to kick an oversized pebble, but cringed in pain when she did. Jumping from one foot to the other, she concocted some sort of ceremonial dance. "OW! Your stupid snake broke my toes." She let out an exasperated sigh and screamed. "I'm going back to my tree. That's where you can find me when you decide to follow through on your deal." Just when she thought they'd all disappeared, she felt a stinging thump of a single pebble on her rump and heard laughter.

CHAPTER 42

Kat leaned against the tree and listened for the sounds of the woods. She might as well have listened for Santa's sleigh bells in August, because the forest remained silent. Although the evening was clear, revealing a sky full of stars, Kat saw no animal movement. Any fireflies had turned off their lights. The wind rustled the leaves, but no crickets played and frogs did not sing. Even the mosquitoes were quiet, but she felt them. Her skin stung from slapping herself to avoid having her blood sucked. Each time she tried to hit one, she only hit herself and the skin was left painful from the bite and slap. A few times she heard giggles.

In a teensy-weensy way she was thankful for the mosquitoes and the tormenting little People. The eerie stillness resurrected every horror movie she'd ever seen. What was she doing in the woods by herself anyway? After a couple of hours crept by with all the hurry of an oozing sore, she turned the ringer of her phone back on in hopes of hearing a human voice. Even more ugly reactions from her Glamour would be better than waiting under the tree watching gruesome images in her mind—she could look in the mirror if she wanted to see that.

Her phone immediately rang. She jumped, wincing when she saw her wart-covered hand grip the phone in the moonlight.

Controlling her voice to sound perky, she couldn't hide that it shook. "Hi. This is Kat, the Glamour Guru. I'll help you make what's not—hot."

"Kat, where are you? I thought we had a date tonight." Duncan's words melted into her ear. The hint of concern in his voice brought forth a new rush of tears, then sobs. "Kat?" He paused while she filled his ear with more sobs. "Kat! Are you okay? Where are you?" She imagined him standing in front of her dark house.

"I'm here!" She sobbed, "And I'm not okay!"

"Are you hurt? I'm at your house. Are you inside? Kat? KAT?" She heard him beating on what she imagined was the red front door of her home. She thought she heard the wooden "welcome" sign bang into the door. Her mom would be upset if it scratched the paint. Then she heard a sharp intake of air. "Someone's broken into your room—I see the broken window. Kat, where are you? I can help you. Let me know where you are."

It was humid and her t-shirt stuck to her. She took a deep breath and tried to blow her eyebrows out of her eyes. She smelled.

"Stay calm. I'll take care of everything. Where are you?"

Who did he think he was—Batman, Spiderman, or a Jedi? She tried to imagine him in tights.

Forcing a chipper voice, she said, "I'm fine. Don't be dramatic. I'm...safe. Everything is going to be—"

"What?!" Duncan yelled on the other end. "Is this some kind of sick joke? Are you hurt or not?"

Finally able to control her emotions, she spoke calmly. "I'm fine, Duncan. This is not a joke. A lot has happened today, and I can't go out with you tonight." She scratched her forearm and realized a rash had formed. Great.

She heard him utter expletives. "I don't see why not." His voice softened. "You've blown me off a lot, Kat. Are you trying to tell me something?"

Kat's entire body tensed and her mouth went dry. Her shoulders ached. Her stomach felt as if she were going to lose her lunch except she hadn't eaten anything all day. She just remembered she hadn't brushed her teeth, either. "Duncan, you've got it all wrong."

"Do I?" he asked as his voice broke with emotion. "This isn't the first night you've blown me off. You won't even tell me where you are. What am I supposed to think? Are you with some other guy?"

Her body moved forward with her response. "NO!"

"Then where are you?"

Like the woods, her response to him was silence.

He expelled a disgusted laugh. "Kat, if you don't go out with me tonight or at least tell me where you are... how can this, I mean, *we*, go on? I don't see—"

Kat cried, "That's just it! I don't want you to see. I don't want you to see me like this."

"Like what?"

"Listen, Duncan, if I told you where I was, would you promise not to come? Please just respect me on this."

"Kat, if you're in trouble, I'm not leaving you alone." His voice became severe. "*Are* you alone?"

"Sort of."

"Tell me where you are, Kat, or we're done. You're acting weird."

"I'm in the woods." She didn't want him to think about it, so she rushed on. "I don't want you involved, Duncan, but I don't want to lose you either. You mean almost as much to me as my looks, and at the moment I don't look that great." The tears welled up again. "I just don't want you to see me right now, okay?"

Duncan laughed. "Kiddy Kat, don't you read the Hallmark cards?" She could hear him grinning into the phone as his voice soothed her nerves. "Don't you know the sayings? Beauty is in the eyes of the beholder? Beauty blooms from the inside out? Pretty is as pretty does." He said, "Kat, you've got it covered."

She squeezed her eyes shut. "I'm glad you think so, but that's why I don't want you to see me now."

"A pimple doesn't scare me. I'm not like other guys, Kat. Give me a little credit." He hung up.

Tiny giggles drifted through the woods. She yelled, "Shut up!" Kat tried to dial him back, but he didn't answer. She kept trying and trying. Finally, she heard a phone ringing and it was getting louder.

"Stop!" She cried out. "Don't come any closer. I don't want you to see me. And... I don't know if you're safe."

He appeared in silhouette on a small rise about six yards away. His hands rested in his pockets, and he stood, placing more weight on one leg than the other. "Hey," he said slyly and held up his cell phone. "Did you call?"

She couldn't make out his features and Kat knew he couldn't see her, either. If he could, he would have reacted differently. A yelp, perhaps? Running away, maybe? He did neither so she figured she was safe as long as he didn't get any nearer. Kat relaxed a little and admired his long body and broad shoulders.

"Stay right there, Duncan. I mean it. I don't want you near me tonight. I've got to get something done, and I don't know if it'll work out if you're here."

Duncan looked around for another person. "What's up, Kat?" His hands reached for the sky in exasperation. "I don't get it." She imagined him holding the moon like a big basketball. If he could only hurry up and slam-dunk it, this night could be over sooner. "Kat, I'm not leaving here until you tell me what's going on."

She sighed. "I'm not telling you, but you can stay as long as you don't get any closer." Hugging her legs to her chest and resting her ear on her knees, she turned away from Duncan. "If you're going to stick around, you might as well tell me a story."

Duncan was a little apprehensive, but took what he could get. "What kind of story do you want?"

Kat pretended to think, but she wanted to know something in particular. "Do you know any stories about what happens to humans who tick off the Little People?"

Duncan sat down on the field grass and crossed his ankles. "Just one really."

"I'm listening," said Kat.

CHAPTER 43

"My grandfather was about our age when it supposedly happened." Duncan began, his voice as clear as the sky. "He and some buddies were hanging out at Three Corners." Kat knew the place. Guys still went there today to race cars and guzzle beer. "One of them started talking about the Little People. I never knew exactly what was said, but they weren't respectful." He paused. "Anyway, out of nowhere this owl flew down in the center of them. A couple of guys got scared. Some even went home. The owl just stayed there in the center, staring at them all."

"Why were they scared of a bird?"

"A lot of cultures see owls as bad luck. You know that short story in the junior lit. book about the owl calling that guy's name?"

She raised an ugly, yet deeply shadowed, hand and waved it. "Um, not a junior yet."

"Oh, yeah. Well, not to ruin the story for you, but an owl calling someone's name is a death omen."

Kat snorted. "Good thing they don't speak English, then."

Duncan paused. "Grandpa didn't leave that night. And, kind of like you, he wasn't scared of the owl. Not then. He didn't respect it either." His voice grew solemn. "It's important to respect nature, Kat."

"The story?" Kat retorted.

"As I was saying, you ought to respect nature. Grandpa didn't. When the owl started its dance...." Duncan waited for her to make a remark, but she didn't. She was biting her tongue to keep from saying something about a bird getting "jiggy." He repeated, "When the owl started its dance, Grandpa made fun of him. He laughed and threw rocks at him. The bird finished its dance and flew away. My grandfather didn't feel bad about the way he acted until he woke up the next morning."

Kat touched her face. "What happened?"

"His face was scarred. It looked like acne scars to everyone else, but he'd never had a skin problem. The scars looked like claw marks to him. He told his parents what had happened. They decided the owl had been a medicine man in disguise sent by the Little People."

Kat's throat constricted and she felt bile rise. She forgot she was hiding her face from him and looked toward him. "Did the... scars go away... *ever?*"

She watched Duncan's silhouette shake his head.

Realization clicked in Kat's head and she brightened. "Hey, I asked about Little People, not medicine men!"

"I know," he replied. "The medicine man was a Little Person. He'd changed shape."

She remembered how the captives had changed colors according to their surroundings. Could they change shapes, too?

Kat threw up. As her body convulsed, trying to purge something from her system besides terror, she began to cry. Her hair fell forward and she struggled to pull it back. She was tired. She was smelly. She was ugly. And she was screwed.

She felt Duncan's hands pulling back greasy strands of her unruly hair. Her body calmed. She wiped her mouth, embarrassed her boyfriend had seen her hurl. Then she became more embarrassed when she realized he could see her now too if she looked at him. This would probably be the last time he would ever be this close to her again. She flung herself into his arms, buried her face in his shoulder, and said, "You know they're real, don't you?"

He smoothed her hair, or tried to at least, and said, "Yeah, I think I do." He squeezed her a little tighter and said, "It's like we talked about before. The stuff that is real isn't always visible." He kissed the top of her head and whispered, "Kind of like lo…"

What was he going to say? Was he about to tell her he loved her and stopped? If she was ever going to hear it from anyone, it would be now. She was definitely too ugly to hear those words after anyone got a glimpse of her. Hmmm. She could always try the Internet dating thing….

"Kat, what is this?" He released her and raised his hand to the tree. His hand fell on the bark of the tree and he read it like Braille. His fingers traced it as if it were wounded.

Kat tucked her head to allow a shield of hair to fall between them as she looked at what he was touching. Then she broke into a smile. "Oh! That." She felt the warmth come to her cheeks. "I did that before we even started dating. I didn't even know you'd noticed me."

Shock registered on his face. "You *carved* our initials in a *tree?*"

"Yeah?" She realized he hadn't seen her face, but he still seemed angry with her.

"Why would you do that, Kat? It's a living being. That's… that's just cruel."

Kat grunted. "I didn't realize you were so granola, Duncan. Besides, I didn't think you'd ever see it anyway. It's no biggie."

His volume grew with each sentence. "No biggie? Kat, you just don't get it. It doesn't matter I might never have seen it. It's here. The damage is done. You've hurt nature. What else have you done I don't know about?" His voice became calmer. "I realize it seems I'm overreacting, but I don't feel I know you and I thought I was falling—," he reached up to brush her hair from her face. A moonbeam shone through the leaves directly on her face. It was so bright she squinted. He stumbled back, falling against the tree trunk.

He whispered the words, "Who *are* you? What have you done?"

His expression of fear prodded more tears from Kat's eyes. A silent frog leapt from behind a tree and peed on her arm. She flung her arm to get rid of it, but it had already jumped away. She was so caught up in wiping away the urine that she almost didn't see when an owl swooped between Duncan and Kat. It clutched her satchel in its talons and flew. She heard the little People in the woods cheer. Duncan jumped and said, "What's that?" but his eyes were glued to the bag as its contents wiggled through the air.

Kat waved it away and yelled, "Fine! Take your little brats back. They talked too much anyway."

Duncan gaped at her as another owl swooped in and flew away with the Wal-Mart sack full of food. She yelled after it, too. "You don't have to steal it. I was going to give it to you!"

The forest came to life. All that had been quiet burst with sound. All that had been still now mobilized. From behind trees and leaves and blades of grass little fairies glowed, illuminating a small area of the forest.

Blaezi stepped into the circle of light. "Exactly, Kat. That's what we thought. You didn't have to steal our Glamour. I offered to share it with you in exchange for food.

"I brought you food, but the bird took it!" cried Kat as she crumpled to the forest floor.

She turned to Duncan, who stared at her with disgust. She reached for his leg, but he stepped back from her. "Help me! All of my dreams had come true and now they're nightmares!"

Duncan shook his head. "I can't help you with that. I had nothing to do with it." He repeated to the multitude. "I had nothing to do with this."

Blaezi said, "We know. But we do want you to come back tomorrow with her," she motioned toward Kat, "and that natural girl who fell in the water."

"Bunny?" he asked. "Bunny's not even here. She's in Australia or something."

"I'm sure you'll manage it." Blaezi smiled at him. "You may go now."

Before departing, Duncan said to Kat." I wish you hadn't done it, Kat. I thought you were different."

She smirked, her teeth yellow. "Don't you see, Duncan? I am." She waved him away. "Didn't you hear? You can go now."

Duncan sprinted back to his car and revved the engine in record time.

Blaezi flew close to Kat's nose. "I believe we have some negotiations to finish."

CHAPTER 44

Blaezi looked up at the shining orb in the night sky. It was the second moon since her exile. Taking a deep breath, Blaezi tried to sound threatening. "For stealing our People, you have been punished. You are the ugliest creature ever to walk these woods."

Kat cowered, dejected against the tree. A whimper escaped her lips, and the People tittered.

Blaezi continued. "If you want to return to your former appearance, you must do as I say."

Kat's head shot up and her wet eyes pleaded with Blaezi. "You mean... I won't be like this forever?"

"Of course you will, you ditzlesnit!" Blaezi laughed. "Unless you do as I say." She snapped her fingers at Kat. "Pay attention." Blaezi sent a rush of Glamour toward Kat and ziddled a wart on her nose. Kat's eyes crossed as she tried to see it. Her fingers caressed the skin where a wart the size of a lima bean rested a moment before. Now, it was gone.

Kat shouted. "I'll do anything! Tell me what to do so I can look like I did before!"

Blaezi said, "It's easy." Blaezi counted off the tasks on her fingers. "All you have to do is bring us food for the rest of your life. Deposit it at this tree. Don't worry. *You* don't have to always do it, but make sure it's here—and don't tell anyone why you're doing it. In exchange, we'll give you portions of Glamour." She looked back at her lush, colorful tail. "Not my whole tail as I offered you before, of course. Nah, you missed your chance on that, but we'll still give you portions." She pursed her lips, looked up, and thought of the Fayes. "Oh! And you need to take food to the far creek for the rest of this summer."

Blaezi smiled. "The last part is the most fun." Blaezi ziddled Kat's eyebrows so she could see her better.

"Fun?" Kat asked without having to squint under a long, furry unibrow.

"Oh, yes," said Blaezi. "Fun for us to watch how you do it." She shrugged, pretending indifference. "It may not be as much fun for you, though." She ziddled another wart.

"Anything!" repeated Kat as she touched her lump-free skin.

"Humans are destroying our home." She patted Kat on the cheek. "You understand how cruel they can be." Blaezi turned to pace in front of Kat's eyes as she spoke, causing Kat to look left and then right. "The *fun* part is *you* have to make them stop." Hovering before Kat, she leaned forward and emphasized the next sentence by poking her in the nose with a tiny finger. "You're going to make them leave our forest as it is—and you're going to make them do that by tomorrow's moonrise."

"But..." Kat sputtered. "I can't do that!"

Blaezi shrugged her shoulders and flew away a few feet before turning around and saying, "Oh, but you have to." She placed one fist on her tiny hip, and with the other, she motioned towards Kat. "Unless you want to look like *this* for the rest of your un-Glamorous life."

Kat was more miserable than she had been before. "How am I supposed to get any of that done looking like this?"

Blaezi cocked her head to one side and pulled on her ear. She nodded to a group of Naturals on a branch directly above Kat. On her command, they wiggled their tails. Glamour rained on Kat, restoring her original appearance.

"Thank you!" gushed Kat. "Thank you so much. I'll do everything I can to get this done for you. I promise."

"Good," said Blaezi before her tone turned icy. "Because if you don't, you'll forever look worse than you did today beginning at nightfall tomorrow." She smiled and said, "Or should I say 'today'?" Blaezi wiggled her wings and flew to the edge of the woods as the sun began to rise. She called back at Kat as she pointed at the rosy colors of morning creeping across the horizon. "You better get going. Sunlight's draining. Oh, and one more thing."

"Yeah?" Kat grumbled.

Blaezi sniffed the air. "Bathe. You smell like frog pee."

CHAPTER 45

On the way back to her house, Kat was nearly hit in the head by her satchel falling from the sky. A hawk circled above her and flew away. Inside was everything that she'd put in there—except the three fairies. She slipped it over her shoulder and compiled a mental list of all she needed to do today.

First, take food to the river and creek. Easy. She'd load up a couple of sacks before her parents got home and take them with her when she returned to the woods tonight. Second, get the builders not to destroy the forest. No water front homes. She had her work cut out for her. She tried to remember the last thing the fairy had requested. She took a deep breath and made a face. Oh yeah. Third, take a shower. She couldn't believe how putrid she smelled from one little frog.

Frog. That's it!

She flipped open her cell phone and dialed. "Mrs. Herrald? Kat Bonner. Have I got a story for you!"

***

Across Eastern Oklahoma, people tended to their morning rituals. Some applied make-up as they watched the news while others drank coffee or ran on treadmills as they watched the morning reports. Most importantly, people were watching the news.

The opening credits had not rolled when the anchor read a piece of paper and said, "This just in. Breaking news from Forrester, Oklahoma. Eve Herrald is on the scene. Eve, what's going on?"

Television screens revealed a thick mass of trees, then cut to Herrald, standing beside a wheeled excavator, one elbow propped on the shoveling device, the other hand gripping the microphone. "Good morning. I know our audience is unaccustomed to seeing me in the morning newscast, but I just couldn't resist this story. Kat Bonner called to tell me about a discovery. The world knows her as the Glamour Guru. After today, though, my bet is she'll be known as Kat the Krusader."

The angle widened to reveal Kat holding a vivarium containing two frogs. She flashed a smile and the audience melted. "Mrs. Herrald, I'm thrilled to be here." Her expression changed immediately as she gazed with a serious expression into the camera as it focused in for a close up. "I have exciting and potentially devastating news." She turned on cue to another camera that had a shot including the vivarium. "In my arms I hold a secret—a new species of frog."

"How did you discover it, Kat?"

"This summer I took a zoology class and we had to create an ecosystem for our final project. My teacher told us he thought it was a new species." She looked into the camera and spoke with conviction. "And it is."

"How do you know?"

"Nowhere is a creature like this documented."

"What's so special about it?"

"Most frogs acquire their food by capturing it with their tongue. Somehow, almost magically, this frog manages to acquire food—without a tongue."

"How do you know it isn't a fluke? A freak of nature like a person born with extra fingers or something? Why are you *certain* that there are more like this one?"

"No one considered it a 'fluke' when a fluorescent purple toad and twenty-three other species were discovered in Suriname." Kat smiled at Herrald. "I've played with many, many of this species during my childhood. I know for a fact there are more where this came from." Crocodile tears welled up in her eyes. "I'm truly thankful I've found them."

"We have a lot to be thankful for here in Forrester."

Kat said to Herrald, "Yes, yet long before Thanksgiving, these gentle creatures will no longer have a place to live." She sighed and forced some tears down her cheek. She tenderly placed the frogs on the bucket of the tractor and motioned toward the forest. "This land will soon be *developed* into a housing addition. The habitat for this undocumented species of frog as well as many other species—perhaps undiscovered—will be destroyed. It's up to Forrester to do something about it." She looked at the camera. "Instead of building homes, we should preserve the homes already there by making it a nature preserve."

"Kat, you're known for creating beauty. Are you interested in science, too?"

Kat twirled her blond hair, charming viewers and endearing herself to the camera so much so that this snippet of film would show nationwide in a matter of hours. "Oh yes. Think about it. I love beauty. If I love beautiful things, I have to love nature too, don't I?" She cocked her head. "That's where the magic of natural beauty begins." Again, her smile captivated.

Mission accomplished.

CHAPTER 46

It was past the heat of the day, but the sun had not set. It was that time of afternoon when both the sun and moon share the heavens.

"I thought I'd find you here." Thorne flew up to the tree and sat on a branch.

Blaezi reclined on the same branch, her eyes focused on the sky. Her voice was faint. "Yeah, I'm here."

"I wondered if you wanted to go with me and see what sort of special foods had been harvested for tonight's festival."

"No thanks." She blinked a lot. "I'll just wait here. I don't have anything to celebrate." She paused. "Not yet."

"Sure you do. You've done so much to help the Naturals." Thorne moved closer to her so that he could make eye contact, but she just looked away.

Laurel, Dogwood, Dion, Diana and others noisily arrived at the tree and made themselves at home on various branches. Their laughter indicated they were much better.

Blaezi sat up and rubbed her face. When she lowered her hands, she wore a huge smile. "I'm so glad you all are safe!" Dion and Diana tackled her and they began a tickle fight until Blaezi begged for mercy.

Wiping away tears from the tickle torture and beginning to control her laughter, Blaezi looked at Dion. He pulled her hair. "Why the sad face? We're here. You should be happy."

Diana pushed him so hard he lost his balance and fell off the branch. Once he'd flown back up to them, he shouted, "Diana?! Is there something I don't know about girls that depresses them? If so, leave me out... but stop pushing me around."

Diana lowered her voice to what she thought was a whisper, yet since she was yelling it, all the others heard her. "Don't be such a ditzlesnit, Dion! Look at the moon!"

A chorus of tiny faces raised their eyes to the sky and they saw it was no longer full.

"Sorry, Blaezi," Dion said. "I didn't even notice."

Diana was still angry at him. "Yeah, just like you didn't notice when that human caught us. Just like you didn't notice a full moon had already passed and Blaezi hadn't come back. Just like you didn't notice when I came up with the great idea to help Blaezi so she wouldn't be permanently banished and you...."

Laurel interrupted. "Did you say, 'banished'?"

Diana's hands were still in mid-story. She looked at him as if he were a slug. "Yeah. I mean, why else would she come here?"

The Naturals chattered. Laurel looked at Thorne and said, "I thought Queen Tania had sent her here to help us."

Dion snorted and gave Diana a playful shove. He spoke out of the corner of his mouth. "In all your wisdom, had you also noticed they didn't know?"

Laurel looked at Thorne who had his arm around the beautiful girl with the long silver tail. She had been a prisoner, but her Glamour was in full glory now. Blaezi hadn't recognized her during the evacuation, but she did now. She was the Natural with the beautiful tail who Thorne had danced with the night Blaezi arrived. She had disappeared the next day. She must have been the one Rock talked about and Thorne never wanted to. She was safe now, though, and even though she'd been ill, her wings' sparkle rivaled the stars.

Laurel's voice sounded injured. "Is this true, T?"

Thorne gave the girl a squeeze and kissed her on the top of her head before releasing her and stepping forward. "It's true she's banished. It's also true Queen Tania sent her here to help us. She had terms. We were part of them. Queen Tania didn't think she could help us, but as we all know, Blaezi tried. I didn't tell everyone before because I didn't think you'd help her if you knew why she had been selected to be the Faye's delegate." He looked everywhere but at Blaezi. He said softly, "It doesn't matter now, though. She had to do it all by the end of two moon's ages. Since her terms haven't been met and the moon is waning, the banishment is official."

Laurel looked at Blaezi and said, "You saved me." He bowed his head and said, "I thought it was because you were my friend— not because you had to."

"I was!" cried Blaezi. "I am!" She looked at all of the People gathered around her. "You all are wonderful. But of course I was trying to meet my terms." She walked up to a tailless Natural. "I wasn't there, but I can identify with some of what you felt when imprisoned in that box. Did you want to go home?"

Still weak, several former prisoners nodded their heads. A few verbalized their agreements.

She clinched both hands into fists and pounded her chest where her heart should be. "I just wanted to find my way home! Can't you understand that? I didn't want you all to know I'd been banished. You accepted me. I was afraid you'd learn my own Fayes didn't want me and decide you didn't want me either."

One of the Naturals in the crowd yelled, "We don't want the Faye's leftovers!" Blaezi found the source of the voice and her eyes met Rock's.

"Well...." Blaezi's eyes rose to the sky again. She swallowed her tears, but they came through. "You won't have to worry about me much longer. Don't worry. I'll finish the deal with the fairy hunter and then I'll leave." Her eyes were ice when she looked at Thorne who had returned to the girl with the silver tail. "I'll leave and everyone will be happier for it. You can return to your perfect little lives where everyone likes each other."

She turned her back to Rock and enclosed Dion and Diana in a hug, complete with wings that wrapped around their bodies. "I'll miss you all. Come visit me when you can. Being a Solitary will be lonely."

Rock interrupted. "As I was saying before being interrupted with..." he made a face like he'd bitten into a wormy apple, "...emotion... we don't want the Faye's leftovers, but the Fayes I'd heard of wouldn't stick around to help friends. Blaezi must be a Natural at heart." He looked at Dion and Diana beside Blaezi. "You're welcome to visit her here anytime. We're having a festival back at the circle when this whole human thing is cleared up if you want to join us tonight."

The crowd glowed with pleasure.

Blaezi tripped over her wings on her way to hug Rock. He offered a hand to help her up. When she was on her feet, instead of hugging her he took her by the shoulders and turned her away, nudging her forward. "There's the human. Go get her."

CHAPTER 47

"Here, let me help you with that." Duncan grabbed a grocery sack Kat cradled in her arms. In both hands, she held other bulging plastic sacks by their handles. She had purchased the food at the farmer's market and trudged across the field from her house to the river.

Kat let him take the bag, but she said, "You don't have to. Really. I've got it covered. I wouldn't want you to go out of your way or anything."

He pulled another bag from one of her hands, grazing her fingers. "I'm here now, aren't I?"

She stopped walking. "Yes. You are." She studied him. "Why are you here?"

"You tell me," he said. Shifting the bags in his hands, he reached for the last one she carried, but she jerked it out of his grasp.

He turned on his heel and continued walking toward the river. "C'mon, you don't want to be late."

Kat had accomplished a lot that day. She'd looked in the mirror more than usual, and each time she looked gorgeous—no signs of warts or other blemishes. Everything was going to work out beautifully. She reminded herself she looked great and business was booming.

Duncan finally spoke. "Pretty smart how you came up with saving the woods."

"Thanks," she said throwing her shoulders back a little with pride. "You told me I was smart once."

"Yeah, I also said you were kind. I guess we can't be right all the time." He shrugged his shoulders. "It looks like some good will come out of this after all."

Kat was shocked. "What do you mean? I'd say that a lot more than some good is coming out of it. Sure, I've done something for the environment, I guess, but I've had a record number of appointments made today. I look fabulous and am going to continue to. What's better, I'm going to continue being able to make other people look fabulous, too." She took a breath and said, "Then, there's you."

He still hadn't looked at her. "Yep. There's me."

Kat couldn't help but wonder. "So, where were you all day?"

"I had a few errands to run."

"Yeah, me too. What'd ya do?"

"I went to the airport for one."

Kat's bag suddenly seemed heavier, and although she knew she was still pretty, she felt less so. She asked, "What could you want at the airport?"

He shifted the bags. "Mrs. Herrald was interviewing you when she was supposed to pick up Bunny. She flew in last night for some reason—wouldn't tell me why. She just left her photo shoots. I guess she missed home or something. Anyway, she called me to pick her up."

Kat snorted. "You'd think she didn't have any friends. Why is she always calling you for help?" As if Kat didn't know.

Duncan said, "No, she has lots of friends. You've got to be one to have them, Kat... as you know. *She's* got plenty of friends."

Ouch. Kat picked up the pace and said, "The tree's right over there. Just set them down and we can wait."

Duncan squinted his eyes and said, "Wait for what? They're already there."

They set the food at the base of the tree, conscious of the

glowing fairies in the branches above them. Blaezi drifted down and rested on Duncan's shoulder. He jumped in surprise, and she reached up to pat his neck. "Don't worry. I'm not going to hurt *you*." Narrowing her eyes, Blaezi's gaze drifted to Kat.

Duncan whispered, "Kat, these aren't the Little People I know."

Kat eagerly held up the items as she listed them. "I brought tomatoes and other fresh produce. I read online you also liked cakes and things, so I brought those, too, and...."

"Stop," Blaezi held up one hand. "Don't do that. Put the food back in the container. It will be easier for us to transport." She snapped her fingers, and owls swooped down, each clasping a side of the plastic bag with their strong talons. The bags vanished in an instant. "Bring paper sacks next time."

Fear filled Kat. What if she brought them food and they were going to mess things up for her anyway? What if she saved their forest and they still sought revenge?

Sitting on Duncan's shoulder, Blaezi dangled her legs, pattering his collarbone with tiny feet. She leveled her gaze at Kat. "You're afraid."

Kat opened her mouth to object but shut it instead. It was too true.

"Good," laughed Blaezi. "You should be."

Kat felt dizzy. She wondered if she were going to faint. Had they put a curse on her? Then her stomach grumbled and she remembered she hadn't eaten since lunch. Courage spoke through her. "I've done what you asked. Are we finished here?"

"Never as long as *you* live," said Blaezi as she smiled. "We're going to get to know each other very well." She stood to whisper in Duncan's ear. Kat couldn't hear and Duncan just nodded. He didn't seem that scared to have a fairy capable of causing great ugliness on his shoulder. Blaezi spoke to Kat. "It's true then? You've done what I've requested. You brought food here and you saved our forest?"

Kat nodded. "I tried."

Blaezi crossed her arms. "Well, you better make sure it works. It looks like it is, though. Our scouts reported earlier that the humans moved out their building equipment. A good omen. Are you responsible?"

Kat nodded again.

Blaezi left Duncan's shoulder to hover in front of his face. "Now, you. You were to bring that other human. Where is she?"

Duncan said, "She volunteered to take food to the creek. I drove her there, but she wanted to walk the rest of the way. She didn't want me to be late."

Kat blurted, "I thought you took the food to the creek. You told me on e-mail you would take care of it for me."

"And I did." He looked her in the eye for the first time that evening. Something was different. "They got their food."

Blaezi clasped her hands together in excitement. "Great! You'll make good worker ants. That's why I wanted you all to meet me. A food supply is too important to leave to an individual. When one requires rest, the others make up for it. What if something were to happen to our fairy hunter?" She considered Kat for a moment and then faked a shudder. "No. We just couldn't have that. So, from now on, you and the other human are responsible for making sure that it gets done, too. We will show our gratitude to you in ways different than with her." Blaezi jerked her head toward Kat.

Duncan seemed surprisingly relaxed. "No problem. Happy to do it."

Blaezi looked as if she found it hard to believe him, but before she could say anything further, a cell phone rang. They all jumped.

Duncan fumbled for his phone and opened it. As he spoke in low tones, Kat alternated between trying to listen in on the conversation and trying to figure out what the tune was. She'd heard it before. From her childhood maybe?

Closing the phone, he said to the People, "Bunny's on her way from the creek." He paused as if unsure of what he was about to say. "She says she's bringing some fairies with her." He looked at Kat as if he couldn't believe what he was going to say next. "One of them claims she's a queen."

Blaezi's wings paled. Her friends swarmed and urged her to retreat to the tree until the queen arrived. Dion flew toward the humans and said, "Stay." Then he disappeared into the shadowed treetop.

Duncan sat on the ground and pressed the heel of his hands to his brow bone. "This is so weird," he muttered.

"Ya think?" Kat asked. "Try having your eyebrows grow together."

He looked at her blankly. "You kind of deserved it."

Ouch again.

"Well," she said as she sat close to him, "there's nothing wrong with me now." She raised a manicured eyebrow in what she hoped was an irresistible expression.

Too quickly he responded, "Yeah, there is, Kat. There always has been. I've just not seen it." He looked at the ground. "You only care about yourself."

"That's not true!" said Kat. Hadn't she done all of this to make everyone prettier? Sure, she was glorified in the process, but she'd just be stupid if she didn't get some recompense. She couldn't find fault with anything she'd done.

Duncan picked up a twig and dug it into the dirt. "It *is* true.

You don't care about Bunny," he said, "and you definitely don't care about me."

"Why would you say that?" Kat noticed his eyes looked wet and his shoulders hung as if he'd missed the winning shot of the state basketball tournament.

He shrugged and she was shocked by his sarcasm. "Gee, I don't know, Kat. Maybe you don't answer the phone. Maybe you break dates. Maybe you are only nice to people if they can do something for you. Everything—friendship, us, whatever—it's always on your terms." He pointed to the glittering tree above them. "Unless you get caught." His lips curled up but the edges of his eyes didn't crinkle the way she liked. "And the saddest thing about it all is you don't even feel guilty about whatever it is you did to them. You only wish they hadn't caught you."

Well, duh. Her stomach grumbled again. Loudly. Why hadn't she eaten? She wanted to change the subject. She didn't want him to hate her. Hadn't Duncan almost told her he loved her? Hadn't he loved her? Almost? She preferred the way he once looked at her before she'd upset him. In the future, she'd have to be more sensitive to people's needs and emotions. Or at least pretend to be.

"I noticed you got a new ring on your phone," she said, hoping to get him to talk about something he liked and stop talking about her.

Duncan nodded, still looking at the ground.

"It sounds familiar, but I can't place it."

"Catchy, isn't it?" He spoke to the ground. "It's from *The Wizard of Oz*, I think."

"I never imagined you as a fan."

He almost grinned.

Relief flooded through her from the break in tension. She

teased, "Which one are you? The Scarecrow? The Tin Man? The Lion? No... wait a minute. I got it. You're the great and powerful Oz!"

He looked at her. "Wasn't he a fake?" He shook his head. "No, Kat. I'm not Oz. I'm not even a fan."

Triple ouchy. One-two-three strikes....

Her hurt feelings came through in her words. "If you're not a fan of *The Wizard of Oz*, then why did you put a song from it on your cell?"

He studied the ground again. "I didn't." He picked up a dandelion.

Then, who did?" Kat feared she already knew the answer.

"Bunny." He blew on the dandelion and white flecks drifted on the air. "When I took her to dinner tonight."

Kat suddenly remembered the tune: *Ding-Dong! The Witch is Dead!*

CHAPTER 48

The congregation beneath the tree saw the glow of Fayes before seeing their bodies. But they saw Bunny first. She had followed the creek to the river and, as she emerged from the woods, a halo of light surrounded her. A multitude of Fayes flew beside her carrying a long train of wildflowers roped together. Attached to the rope was a tiny carriage, glowing brightest of all below a roof of iridescent green.

Duncan and Kat gaped at the parade. Thorne gripped Blaezi's arm and they descended from the tree, leading others. In an instant, luna moths, performing the service of roof to the queen's carriage, flew away. Queen Tania remained seated on a cushioned piece of bark suspended in air. The bodice and skirt of her gown were made of the cool gray feathers of the Mourning Dove while her high collar consisted of the white feathers of Cattle Egrets. A human's "lost" diamond ring crowned her head.

Queen Tania motioned toward Bunny as if she were swatting away gnats. "You may go," she bellowed. Her voice rang through the forest. Most of the Naturals had never heard such ferocity from one of the People, and they trembled almost as much as Blaezi.

Bunny scurried toward Duncan and he embraced her. Kat almost didn't notice because her eyes watched the beautiful spectacle. Blaezi flew to the humans. "We'll see you here tomorrow." She handed Kat a small portion of Glamour and waved them away. They seemed more than willing to oblige. Blaezi returned to Thorne and the others.

"Blaezi, come forward," called Queen Tania.

Thorne attempted to escort Blaezi when she moved toward her queen, but she jerked her arm away from him. "This is my job. You've helped me with everything else. Let me do this alone." He nodded and released her arm.

Blaezi flew before the queen and curtsied. The queen's eyes grazed Blaezi's body from wings—to tail. She didn't appear to like what she saw. The other Fayes noticed the Naturals' tails and a few dropped their flowers.

As was the custom, the queen spoke first. "You have not met your terms of exile."

Blaezi already knew this, so she stood silent.

"Your terms have not been met. You have not even come close to addressing the problem of Blight and Rottus. They have wreaked havoc on the Garden throughout the summer. Obviously, my entire Council has been unable to stop the destruction, so it is inconceivable that you could do anything." She raised her eyebrows and surveyed the Naturals who had just received word of her arrival. "I assume you have helped the Naturals with their problem or they would have banished you, too."

Blaezi opened her mouth to speak, but thought better of it and pressed her lips together.

"Instead of fulfilling your terms, it seems you have done something else." She motioned to Bunny with a lazy wave of her hand. "You sent this human to our realm with provisions." Queen Tania picked at something on her pillow of moss. "For that we are grateful. It is the absolute least you could do since you caused the food shortage." She sniffed. "However, you have placed us in jeopardy once again by letting the humans know our domain.

What have you to say for yourself?"

Blaezi stared silently at Queen Tania for an uncomfortable amount of time before saying, "I've been punished and refuse to allow you to make me feel worse about myself. I know I've not met my terms and accept the consequences. I don't need to explain myself, but you do." The Faye court gasped in unison at this blatant disregard for authority. Blaezi continued. "Why have you come here? To humiliate me? To ensure the Naturals know I'm banished?" She threw her hands up. "Well, they know!"

She soared to Thorne and grabbed him by the elbow and thrust him before the queen. "You sent me with him because you thought it was a joke. You didn't think I could help, but I did. How dare you! They came to us in peace and friendship and asked for our help and you sent them a joke!" She pounded her chest. "Me!" She placed both of her hands on the queen's carriage and leaned forward, tilting it so the queen slid toward Blaezi. "Well, I'm not a joke anymore. I *did* help them." She released the bark so fast Queen Tania bounced up and down as Blaezi twirled around knowing the tip of her long tail brushed the queen's nose. "I helped all of them. The whole forest. In turn, I even helped you."

The queen sneered. "Oh? What have you done?"

"Plenty."

Thorne stepped forward. "For one, she has the humans bringing us food. Also, she has saved the forest—which includes your little area of creek." He looked at the queen with a familiar disdain. "She's done more for me than you ever could."

A frog jumped forward and Dogwood said, "She's helping the frogs. She sent a large group of them your way this morning."

Blaezi put her hands on her hips. "They love slugs."

Laurel spoke up. "She saved me."

One after the other, Naturals stepped forward saying, "And me."

Blaezi stood squarely in front of the queen. "What have *you* done for your Fayes?" She met the queen's steely gaze. "Perhaps you'd like to start by telling us about what you do with their tails?"

The ice from Queen Tania's mood melted. "Now, now, Blaezi. Don't say something you'll regret." The queen moved forward and hugged Blaezi. "It seems I've misjudged you. Perhaps you were misplaced all along as a Garden Guard. Perhaps you should join my Council." She released her hold on Blaezi. "Yes, that should suit you just fine."

Diana squealed in delight as Dion moved forward to congratulate her, but Blaezi took a step back and deliberately blinked her eyes three times. "Are you saying I'm no longer banished?"

Queen Tania said, "You're too good of a Faye." Her smile sparkled with deception. "You're welcome to come home."

Blaezi turned around to look at the others. Dion and Diana were already planning the return trip, but past them, Blaezi saw Thorne's sagging wings. He reached out to pat Laurel and Dogwood on the shoulders. Past them, Rock stared back at her. He shook his head.

Blaezi slowly turned around. "I know," she replied.

"How?" asked the queen. "I just lifted your banishment."

"I know," repeated Blaezi.

The queen demanded, "Then how did you know that before I told you?" She leaned back. "Are you a seer?"

Blaezi made a noise that resembled a hysterical laugh. Dion and Diana stopped gossiping and even the down-trodden Naturals paid attention. "I didn't know you were going to lift it. I said 'I know' because you said that I'm welcome to come home." She looked around her. "I'm already there."

A cold blast of air rushed through the woods. Queen Tania's

nose almost met Blaezi's as she said, "Are you saying you'd prefer to stay with these... these Naturals than return to the Fayes?"

Blaezi didn't back down. "Yes. And I bet others would too if they knew you stole their Glamour."

More gasps escaped the Fayes. Blaezi felt a firm grip on her shoulder and she swung around to meet her assailant. She was met with the wrinkled face of Raine. "We're glad you'll be staying with us, Blaezi." He leaned forward, and Queen Tania allowed him to press his cheek to hers. "Tania." She nodded, some of the anger melting from her face. "Would you like to tell them or shall I?" asked Raine.

Her wings glowed red and she said, "I refuse to listen to this." She turned to Blaezi. "You made a foolish decision." To her caravan, she said, "Return home." They left as quickly as a lightning strike.

Raine placed one arm around Blaezi and turned to the others. "Let's continue this at the festival." Next, he spoke only to Dion and Diana. "You may need to return with your queen now, but you are welcome here anytime."

CHAPTER 49

The drums of the forest festival greeted them long before they reached the People's circle. The few Naturals who had stayed behind welcomed the rest with food and games. After Blaezi ate some watermelon, she flew to Raine on the edge of the clearing. He clasped her hand when she flopped down beside him.

"You have come for the rest of the story," he said instead of asking.

"Absolutely," she replied. "What does Queen Tania do with all of our tails?" She lowered her voice. "And how do you know?"

The skin around Raine's eyes creased as deeply as water ripples when he laughed. "I have known Tania for many moons."

"And that's another thing. You're the only one who ever calls her that."

"What?"

Blaezi looked around before whispering, "Tania."

Raine laughed again. "It's her name, isn't it?"

Blaezi tugged on her ear. "Yeah, but everyone else puts the queen part first."

"I see," said Raine. "I knew her before all of that business."

Blaezi asked, "You mean, you knew her before she was queen?"

Raine nodded.

"You remember when she was born? When she slid down a moonbeam?"

"Oh no!" Raine chuckled. "I'm not as old as all that."

Blaezi's ear was sore from her tugging on it in concentration.

Raine said, "She's much older than I am."

"What? How?!"

Raine shrugged. "I was a bit of a young Natural when the Fayes came to our forest. I admired her. She was a good leader among her People. Because she led them to safety..." he grinned, "... and was fortunate enough to meet me to teach her the ways of this world, they named her queen." He threw his bark-like hands in the air. "The rest is lore!"

"No, it's not," pressed Blaezi. "First of all, why did you help her? Second of all, how could she look younger than you if she's older?"

He squeezed her hand. "My dewdrop, she was beautiful—as she is now. Of course I was going to help her. As for how she seems younger than I... well, you wondered what she did with all of those tails."

Blaezi swallowed a sob. The Fayes' tails had been sacrificed all their lives—just to give Queen Tania Glamour. She was no better than the fairy hunter.

Blaezi found her voice. "When did you learn she wasn't as good as she appeared?"

"One evening giggling little People bounded into our laps from the moonbeam."

Blaezi recalled the lore and curled her lips in distaste. "You kissed her?"

He nodded. "She is a much better queen than mother," he said sadly. "Let's talk about you. I heard you had a reading before you came here."

Blaezi nodded, trying to think back that far.

Raine said, "Well, the reader's words convey truth." He looked out at the dancers and Blaezi's eyes followed his. They rested on Thorne and that pretty Natural. They looked up at the same time. Raine waved and they waved back. Thorne grabbed the girl's hand and the couple flew toward them.

Blaezi didn't want them to come near her. She had forgotten all about the girl and her tail. She thought of Dion. Maybe she should have gone back to the Fayes. He was a nice Faye. She looked at Thorne. Of course, Dion wasn't Thorne. She looked at Raine. And Raine wasn't Tania.

The girl arrived breathless, her tail fluttering. Raine clasped their hands simultaneously and departed without a word.

Thorne yelled as if he were still on the dance floor. "I just realized I never introduced you two! Blaezi, this is Rose!"

Thorne. Rose. A perfect pair.

Blaezi ignored the introduction. "Raine and I were just talking about the reading I had at Midsummer Festival. I can't remember what she said."

Rose spoke up. "Oh! That's easy. I'll be right back."

Thorne watched her disappear. "Rose is a reader, too."

Of course.

"I'm glad you were almost banished from the Fayes," Thorne said. "If you hadn't come, I might never have seen her again."

Blaezi had trouble looking at him. "I'm glad I could make everyone happy."

Rose returned with a firefly. She held it as tenderly as the Faye reader had held the ladybug. She caressed the gleaming insect until her hands glowed with its light. From the light shone the scene of the reader telling Blaezi her fortune, but neither Thorne nor Blaezi could hear it. Rose could, however, and she giggled as if it were a joke. At the end of the reading, the image vanished from the air and returned to the lightning bug. She patted it on the rump and it flew on its way.

Rose said, "It does seem that your reading is true."

Thorne looked irritated. "She doesn't remember what it is. Since you know, do you want to stop teasing her and tell?"

Blaezi was able to smile. Maybe he wasn't so enamored with Rose after all.

"Oops. Sorry." She flipped her long tail and sat down. "Well, you did need to use extreme caution with the human, and your work did send you away—all the way here."

Blaezi nodded. She remembered that part.

"Your loyalties have definitely been revealed to all. I mean, lots of Fayes and Naturals heard you tell the queen of the Fayes you were already home. That was great."

"Oh, yeah." Blaezi remembered that part, too.

"And you had one chance to find home—which you did—but you didn't know the way when you started."

Blaezi nodded again, remembering all of this. "It seems like there was something else, though."

"That's the best part." She grinned. "'Danger is near you, but trouble will be your guide, salvation and destiny.'" Thorne grinned too, but his wings turned pink as he refused to look at Blaezi. Rose playfully shoved him.

"What?" demanded Blaezi. "This isn't fair. I don't get it. Why do I want trouble to be my destiny? How is that funny?"

Rose flung her arm around Thorne's shoulder. "Do you know why they call him T?"

Blaezi said, "Because it's the first letter in Thorne."

Rose cocked her head to one side. "Did you ever notice that most Naturals don't spell?"

Blaezi jerked her head back. She hadn't noticed. 'T' is a human letter and only Fayes spell in English. She asked, "How do you guys know it? You don't speak English."

Thorne looked at Blaezi. "No, but our mother did."

Their *mother*? *Their* mother spoke English?

Blaezi rushed in. "You told me that Queen Tania sent help because she owed you."

Thorne nodded. "She owes *us*."

"Had you ever lived with the Fayes before?"

Rose said, "No. We've always lived with the Naturals. Our mother is a Faye. She claimed we were too in touch with the Natural world, especially Thorne. She disliked him so much she began calling him *T*."

Thorne shrugged at Blaezi. He spoke softy. "She said it was short for *Trouble*."

Rose stood up. "I think I'll leave you two to your destinies." She flew off to the dancers.

The shelter of the thick forest shadowed the edge of the clearing. If it hadn't, a moonbeam might have revealed Thorne and Blaezi. They were close enough to kiss.

EPILOGUE

Much softer than any others on the market, the makeup brushes sparkled. They clinked almost musically in the glass cylinder where she stowed them. She dusted the excess powder from the counter into her cupped hand, returned it to its jar, and smiled.

Kat loved being featured in all of the fashion magazines. *Seventeen* claimed that dermatologists were not needed if Kat the Krusader of Beauty was near. "With a swish of her makeup brush, blemishes disappear—as if by magic." Although they never listed her ingredients, *YM*, *Vogue*, and *Cosmo* hailed her "all natural" beauty products. *Marie Claire* ran a special article about her days spent in the rain forests. Most of the world thought she was a tree-hugger because she trekked into the woods on private expeditions and returned with new beauty tricks. Even Oprah and Barbara Walters interviewed her on their daytime shows. ABC had offered Kat her own beauty talk show. *Teen People* featured her in their "most beautiful" issue and hired her to do the makeup for all of the other celebrities photographed. Her "friends"—and thanks to Duncan's illuminating revelation, she'd acquired many who thought she was one—adored her and were very useful.

She was known as the Glamour Guru. Her work seemed to magically conceal the ugly warts of society and bring out its allure. Of course, her products could never be mass produced and sold on the home shopping networks. They could never bear the label claiming nothing was "harmed in the making of this product."

If she'd felt guilty, Kat would have comforted herself at night knowing she made the world a prettier place.

But who needs guilt when you've got Glamour?

BOOK CLUB QUESTIONS
FOR GLAMOUR

1. At the beginning of the novel, Blaezi is more consumed with enjoying herself than anything else. How does she change as the novel progresses? What does she learn?

2. Kat is evil in many ways. Does she have any redeeming qualities?

3. When Queen Tania keeps her people's tails, she steals their power, their Glamour—their freedom. In what ways can a leader steal someone's freedom?

4. The repeated reappearance of the number two suggests the motif of mirror images and reflection. Can you find characters or situations that are paired to illustrate this idea?

5. Rock, Laurel and Dogwood are the three tribes of Cherokee Little People. The tribes have distinct characteristics. Rock can be threatening if their territory is invaded. Laurel is fun loving and likes to play tricks. Dogwood is fair and often helps people. In what ways are the characters like the tribes they were named after?

6. Consider fairy tales. Do characters in *Glamour* resemble the archetypical characters of fairy tales (witch, princess, prince,

damsel in distress, mischief-maker, etc)? Who are they and how are they like other fairy tale characters? How are they different?

7. The Naturals believe that it is important to be connected to nature. They believe extended removal from nature can make one lose touch with what is important. Is this true? Give examples for your reasons.

8. The Fayes change who they are in an attempt to protect themselves. Is this a good decision? Why or why not?

9. Many cultures have their own version of Little People. *Glamour* takes place in eastern Oklahoma. Would the story have worked as effectively in another setting? If so, where and why?

10. The study of the moon is vital to many ancient civilizations. It is believed that the new moon is a time where a new cycle begins. During a full moon, the fullness of what was wrought during the last new moon is brought to light. The waning crescent is a time of rebirth. How are Blaezi's actions reflected in this cycle?

For more information please visit my website:
www.brandibarnett.com
or email me at:
brandi@brandibarnett.com